Who Will Die Last

Judaic Traditions in Literature, Music, and Art
Ken Frieden and Harold Bloom, *Series Editors*

Other Books in Judaic Traditions in Literature, Music, and Art

Who
Will
Die
Last

Stories of Life in Israel

David Ehrlich
Edited by Ken Frieden

Syracuse University Press

Syracuse University Press
Syracuse, New York 13244-5290

For a listing of books published and distributed by Syracuse University Press, visit our website at SyracuseUniversityPress.syr.edu.

ISBN: 978-0-8156-1019-9

Library of Congress Cataloging-in-Publication Data
Ehrlich, David, 1959–
    [Short stories. Selections. English]
    Who will die last : stories of life in Israel / David Ehrlich ; edited by Ken Frieden. — First edition.
        pages cm. — (Judaic traditions in literature, music, and art)
    ISBN 978-0-8156-1019-9 (pbk. : alk. paper) 1. Ehrlich, David, 1959–
—Translations into English. I. Frieden, Ken, 1955– II. Title.
    PJ5055.2.H47A2 2013
    892.4'36—dc23   2013017811

Manufactured in the United States of America

Contents

Preface

Ken Frieden

You are lucky to be holding this book in your hand or reading it on a screen. Few American readers have had the opportunity to enjoy David Ehrlich's stories, because until now little of his work has been printed in English.* This collection makes available a wide selection of Ehrlich's stories, most of which were first published in Hebrew and appeared in his books *Ha-bekarim shel shlishi ve-hamishi* (Tuesday and Thursday Mornings; Tel Aviv: Yedi'ot aharonot, 1999) and *Kahol 18* (Blue 18; Tel Aviv: Yedi'ot aharonot, 2003).

The stories in *Who Will Die Last* are a milestone of cultural transfer. Israelis know Ehrlich both as a fine author and a moving force in the ongoing literary life of Jerusalem. His bookstore café Tmol Shilshom has become an important site, where prizewinning books—like Nathan Englander's

---

* One rare exception was the inclusion of his astonishing text "The Store" in Michael Gluzman and Naomi Seidman's anthology *Israel: A Traveler's Literary Companion* (San Francisco: Whereabouts Press, 1996).

For the Relief of Unbearable Urges—have been written, and it is a favorite venue for literary events. Readings by eminent authors such as Yehuda Amichai, Aharon Appelfeld, David Grossman, Batya Gur, Etgar Keret, Zeruya Shalev, and A. B. Yehoshua have been hosted by Tmol Shilshom. In his own fiction, David Ehrlich has echoed, combined, and transformed features drawn from many of these innovators.

While I was editing *Who Will Die Last*, I was reminded of Isaac Babel's story "Guy de Maupassant." Babel's narrator describes the work of translating and editing: "When a phrase is born, it is both good and bad at the same time. The secret of its success rests in a crux that is barely discernible. One's fingertips must grasp the key, gently warming it. And then the key must be turned once, not twice."** As editor, I took the liberty of turning some words and phrases by the many talented translators who produced this volume of David Ehrlich's stories. Babel's narrator goes on to restate the secret of translation when explaining the art to his beautiful but inept collaborator: "I spoke to her of style, of an army of words, an army in which every kind of weapon is deployed. No iron spike can pierce a human heart as icily as a period in the right place."

All of the translators who made this volume possible have labored admirably to transfer the aura and graphic details of Ehrlich's fiction into English. As one of the few people who have had the privilege to read all of these stories in both languages before their publication here, I have strived to make certain that nothing is lost in translation—or at

---

** Isaac Babel, *The Collected Stories*, ed. Nathalie Babel, trans. Peter Constantine (New York: Norton, 2002), 445.

least to ensure that where something has been lost, something else has been gained. In my editing I have not tried to smooth out rough edges or to craft the stories to sound the same, because they are narrated by many distinctive characters with dissimilar voices. Moreover, good translators like these also have voices of their own that should not be suppressed. As a result, the diversity of translators corresponds indirectly to the many voices of David Ehrlich's fiction.

You will encounter surprising twists and turns as you move through this volume. In advance, I only want to promise that a slow and attentive reading will repay your efforts. There is a searing honesty in Ehrlich's vision, matched by his concise style and subtlety. He has imagined so much, before and behind the scenes, that a novel or a screenplay could be written from each individual story. Take your time; there is no hurry. Ehrlich is waiting patiently for you to join him so that he can guide you on a mystery tour of his imaginary world, which offers a safe place to explore a set of alternate realities.

If you know Israel well, it will return to you in these stories with a kind of alienated majesty. If you have never visited Israel or the Middle East, let this be your introduction to an enigmatic country that is as magical as it is haunted by harsh realities.

Who Will Die Last

To the Limit

Translated by Charlie Buckholtz

left a meeting in Ashkelon at 3:30, and at the first intersection a red Lantis tried to pass me on the right. Usually I let people pass instead of getting into a fight, but this guy pissed me off. In the side-view mirror I could see his gaudy, orange shirt and gelled hair, and so I kept going fast—I was not letting this guy in. When his lane ended he had no choice but to get in behind me. He didn't leave it at that, the bastard, and wanted me to move out of his way—yeah, right!

Next he tried to pass on the left, but that wasn't in the cards: in the left lane a bus was right behind me, so he ended up stuck behind the bus. I could see even from a distance how much this burned him. I knew he wasn't really in a hurry, that something inside him was rushing, so I didn't let him pass me on the right or left. He kept trying and pushing at all the exits, all the way to Tel Aviv, and I didn't let him. We did a kind of dance on the highway. Even though I needed to get off at Ginot, he pissed me off so much that I decided to continue one more exit north. This time I did it to spite him: slowed down, and—every time he came to pass me—sped up. I was tired of the game but I was trapped, so I continued one more exit north, just to show him, one last time.

We almost had an accident on the exit ramp, and when he finally started honking, other drivers started to notice our little happening. But what could I do? I felt I had an obligation, called my wife, and told her I was held up at work. We continued until the Country Club exit, where we got off to take a leak. We parked close enough not to break contact but far enough apart not to have to speak, and we kept track of each other in the bathroom. Then we went back to our cars, pulled out at exactly the same time, and continued that way to the Pancake Place, where we stopped to eat. Just because you're suffering from road rage on the highway doesn't mean you have to stay hungry. By then we could already read each other and knew we were going with this to the limit.

So we sat at the same table.

Afterward we got up and left at the same time, and gave *Wow!* what a show all the way to Haifa. We freaked everyone out with our tire screeching.

But I managed not to get distracted by the good feeling I'd developed for him in the Pancake Place. I focused on my anger at this idiot who was holding me up for so long on the road, and I remembered that all of it was because he had tried to pass me on the right. We continued like this for another hour, which got more difficult with the traffic jams in Haifa, but we were obliged to continue. From Checkpost North we crawled past a few exits side by side—he was ahead in the left lane, or I was ahead in the right lane—each time waving hello. When we got out of the Krayot suburbs, things became easier but also more dangerous on the two-lane road. In my excitement I forgot how the road went, and *boom!* We hit the northern border, the country ended, and we stood there gasping beside the cars.

We knew it would never be this good again.

The Store

Translated by Naomi Seidman

When Micha Rothman and his group founded our village eighty-two years ago, not a single road in Palestine had been paved yet, and hardly anyone had settled to the north and east. Once every day or two, a horseback rider or carriage would pass along the road, and everyone would gather around to hear the news and gossip from Jaffa and from the other villages.

Peace and quiet, that was our character throughout the years. Quiet, and hard work, and lending a hand when it was required, but also carefully guarding one another's privacy, each of us minding our own business.

We take pride in that.

With all due modesty, it should be noted that our village thrived and prospered beyond the expectations of its founders. There was no farm in the village that did not supply the Tnuva company with fine milk, excellent eggs, or lusciously sweet fruit. There was no home that did not raise three or four children, most of whom returned here immediately after their army service without descending into drugs or dangerous treks through jungles. Even during the worst of the economic recession of the eighties, we were far from financial ruin. No one went into debt, no one asked for help.

Even when they built the new highway, which passed literally meters from the Barkays's back fence, we weren't much affected. Villages less solidly rooted than our own went through difficult transitions when the wave of modernization washed through their streets. But in our case, either because of our lack of interest in the world or because of the world's lack of interest in us, the atmosphere of the good old days lingered, and each of us held our own against the evil winds that blew. Even when the trucks barreled past, hauling their loads back and forth, perpetually delivering newspapers that had more colors than news, even then we could hear, beyond the roar, the rustle of the wings of birds that still remembered that, once, there were swamps here.

And then Lucy Galili died. Lucy, Elchanan's widow, was stronger than steel, with roots that were deeply and firmly planted, and the spark in her eyes seemed to have leapt from one generation to another, radiating wisdom and experience since the days of Adam.

The only thing was, they had no children.

Immediately after the funeral the great dispute over their house began. Some of us wanted to put in a library, a few suggested a small museum, and others thought that we should build a synagogue on the property.

But before the dispute could really heat up, to everyone's amazement, a relative suddenly appeared. Needless to say, this person had never set foot in the village during the long lifetime of the Galilis. Moreover, there were some who remembered Lucy explicitly stating that she had no family, anywhere. But unfortunately this man, who was wearing what was perhaps the first suit that had ever appeared among us, proved that he was indeed a nephew of a cousin of Lucy's who had been killed in the Holocaust. And before we could grow accustomed to the idea and put a stop to the rest of the process, the man entered into a selling frenzy.

It should be understood that none of us had any experience with such matters. We did not know whether we should be taking legal action to try to stop the man, and if so, how to do it, and we also were unsure about the ethical justification for such a step, since, after all, the house did not belong to us.

Now, of course, we regret our inaction.

We regarded with astonishment the cast of characters that walked around and into poor Lucy's house, types we could scarcely believe existed in this country of ours, and wondered what interest they could possibly have in our village. The potential buyers appeared in succession as if in some horror movie, each with his own vision: one wanted to set up a stud farm, the second a restaurant, and the third intended to bring in beehives. What they shared was a basic unsuitability for our village, and also a complete lack of interest in the primary question of whether the inhabitants of the place wanted them or not.

Everything happened very quickly. In the course of two weeks, Elchanan Galili's house had been sold to a couple from Netanya. Rumor had it that the price reached a half million dollars, a purely imaginary sum for most of us. Until that point it had not occurred to any of us that our plots of land had any particular financial value, the whole question of price having been simply irrelevant.

From Uri Samit's nearby porch, we watched them unload furniture from a truck, and then take a stroll around the orchard, and a few days later paint the house a vulgar shade of cream. Every once in a while they waved hello at us. We responded unenthusiastically. At that point we were not yet aware of how careful we had to be with this apparently naïve couple.

After a few weeks, they noticed that they had neighbors. Every day they knocked on someone else's door, introduced themselves, and wanted to have a conversation, it wasn't clear about what. To the best of our knowledge no one responded positively to these belated attempts at neighborliness. It was clear that they wanted something, and whatever that something was, no good could possibly come of it.

That may be why the matter of the store came as such a complete surprise.

One day Ilan, Yossi Amir's younger son, went running through the village calling, "A store, a store," his voice breaking as if someone was trying to murder him. It turned out that, overnight, they had put up a billboard the size of a movie screen by the side of the highway to draw attention and direct traffic to the old Galili house, in which they were selling junk they had acquired the devil knows where.

By the end of the week, more people had wandered around our village than had come through since its founding. In one fell swoop, we had been transformed from some completely anonymous place to a point of interest on the Israeli map, a well-known attraction throughout the region and a necessary stop from anywhere to anywhere. It was impossible to work in the field for more than an hour running without some dubious face popping up before your eyes to ask where the restrooms were, or how much you were selling your house for, or which way was Eilat.

That couple seemed to have a sense for what would sell. We couldn't understand why sane people would stop on their way home from the Sea of Galilee to buy such worthless junk. We snuck in there and were amazed at the illogical assortment of things they were selling: a faded umbrella for twenty shekels, a broken toaster, an old radio with a green light bulb, old records. Everything was in complete disarray, a mishmash of things that people had thrown out. In the middle of this mess they had draped cloths from the East, peacock feathers, broken seashells, and who knows what else. At the far end of the store sat the man from Netanya, solemnly ringing up purchases on his cash register, the bell of which echoed from one end of the village to the other, while the woman roamed importantly among the bargains, tossing around lies about the history of each piece of trash. It was especially nauseating to find Lucy Galili's blue dress in a heap of clothing, and Elchanan's broken pitchfork, and a whole host of other objects that bore so many memories for us, each of which was worth more than the gang that was putting them up for sale.

The main problem that faced us now was the inevitable corruption that awaited our younger generation. For eighty-two years we had been, without being aware of it, a place of peace and quiet, values, and beauty. And now, suddenly, the ground had erupted beneath our feet, and all the filth of the country was breaking into our streets, strolling about our yards without anyone stopping it, threatening to pour its evil stench over everything.

As if in mourning, we gathered to take counsel. Few of us had any ideas. After all, we were practical people, people who worked and toiled, honest and loyal as the day is long. How could we navigate the twisted ways that dominated the landscape over the horizon?

It was decided that we should have a talk with them. Clearly, no one was eager to take the mission upon himself.

Heads bowed, the delegation of three who had been chosen by lot went out to meet the couple from Netanya. It is not difficult to imagine the conversation between them, three older farmers whose strength was in their hands, not their mouths, and the slippery pair who had invaded our lives. "You can live here, that would be fine," someone said, "but you have no right to turn our village into the whole country's whorehouse." The man and woman, for their part, tried to defend themselves with clever talk and with the absurd proposition that they would make a symbolic contribution to the village by erecting a monument to its war dead. The conversation became no more fruitful after continuing for some five minutes. Our people were not swayed by the lady of the house's invitation to have a cup of coffee, and certainly not to sit down, and they left more or less as they had come.

Two days passed and nothing happened. It is hard to believe that those people did not sense the ground burning beneath their feet. The village, like a living, breathing creature, was preparing to vomit them forth, and even if no one expressed it in words, the matter hung in the air as threatening and tangible as a loaded gun.

With no particular ardor and with even less skill, we took the necessary steps. Katz's wife called them up to tell them that they would have to go. Then a note written in unambiguous terms was placed on their doorstep. It was clear that if that did not work, nothing would, and that with every passing day our situation was becoming more dangerous. Nevertheless, we held off for another whole day.

That night, terrible winds blew. As if in response to a call, we all assembled on Uri Samit's porch and gazed sorrowfully into the night. There, in the heart of the darkness, stood the small house, surrounded by an orchard and field and meadow, with a dovecote on the right and an abandoned dog kennel on the left. Because low clouds covered the moon, it all looked like one solid dark mass, whistling in the wind like a horse flute. None of us said a word. There was no plan. With smoldering eyes, we all faced in the same direction, as if everything were perfectly obvious. What remains uncertain is which of us went first, if, in fact, anyone did. But everyone was there, walking into the darkness in a single row, tense and ready. In one motion we all lit matches, in one motion we tossed them into the thorns, and together we stood and watched the fire break out and roll from the field toward the house. From all four directions, the house caught fire and was utterly consumed.

Of course, none of us intended to harm the people inside the house. No one knows why they didn't manage to wake up and escape. Did the fire spread too quickly, or were they under the influence of sleeping pills or drugs or some such thing? Undoubtedly the heaps of junk they kept in their store helped fuel the flames: the cloth went up in smoke as if it had been resigned to ignite, and apparently the proprietors were simply trapped in the flaming inferno.

By the time the firemen arrived, there was nothing for them to do but compliment us on our rapid mobilization in extinguishing the blaze. We thanked them for thanking us and waited for the ambulance to arrive and take the bodies away. Among us passed the thought, unexpressed, that we should report what had occurred, but of course we refrained from doing so.

The police collected evidence for the next two or three days and rapidly came to the conclusion that the fire was probably set by Arabs, one of many such incidents of arson that had been spreading through the country.

We were surprised to learn that the couple from Netanya had no heirs. We were compelled to bury them and say a few nice words ourselves. We waited for a while, convinced that something was about to happen, but nothing did. We took down the sign above the store, rescued what trees we could in the orchard, and finally assembled again to discuss the future of the plot.

Again a few people suggested putting in a library, others, a small museum, and there were those who brought up the idea of the synagogue. But because of a general unwillingness to get entangled in investments, the plot still sits there, abandoned.

Stars

Translated by Shalom Goldman

S o it's that easy in Hebrew, too?" says Steven.
I've just told him the Hebrew word for "no": *lo*. "I told
you it's easy, just make this motion with your mouth, put your
tongue up and purse your lips. That way . . . no . . . that way."

He prefers to make me practice my own language. "Lo,
lo, lo, lo . . . try it, you can do it, believe me, you can . . .
there, you see, I told you that you can do it!"

I give him a hangdog look as he tries to shape my mouth
with his finger—as if he can instill "No" in me from the
outside. But I know why I'm standing there with my mouth
open like a cement mixer. It's his kiss I'm waiting for—and
it comes.

He's teaching me to say "No" because he is sick of all
the Israelis hanging out in our living room. We haven't
yet recovered from the couple that was here last week, and
already there's a call from some people that I don't know—
but they know my brother Amir. Well, they don't exactly
know him—but they'd like to come over on Tuesday, "just
for a couple of days." Once again, I know that it's a bad idea,
but I really don't know how to say no.

11

Steven goes to work and I go for cooking lessons. That's our division of labor: He works and I have a good time. I haven't found work in London, but then perhaps I haven't really looked. The kind of work you can get without a work permit, that's just the kind of work I won't take.

So I'm taking cooking classes—a wonderful way to pass the time. When I get back home I have exactly enough time for my other hobby: an afternoon nap. When I wake up, I cook a four-course meal for Steven and myself.

But today I am not cooking. I have a meeting.

This is the first time I've been back to Heathrow since I arrived last year. I like the excitement that the airport provides; the list of exotic destinations on the "Departures" board gives me a pleasant buzz. But it also makes me anxious: when I take off from here I'll be leaving Steven behind.

But I'm not flying anywhere, at least not today. I'm here to meet someone I don't know, someone who has flown here from Israel to talk to me—and I know exactly what he wants. Amir warned me in a postcard on which he wrote only three lines—the last of which ended with two words: "You decide."

His name is Kobi Levi. I identify him immediately. His sunglasses, resting at a nonchalant angle on his gelled hair, give him away. He's so Israeli. He doesn't recognize me. With his attaché case, his unfashionable tie and sweaty face, he looks totally lost. I don't hurry to rescue him. He scans the people at the bistro in the corner of the terminal and sees no one who could be me; his glance passes over me without stopping. I have a very ordinary face. I had told him that I would wear a jeans jacket, but this morning I didn't feel like putting on anything more than a T-shirt.

He's wearing a suit and has on sunglasses—two things you don't need on a day like this in London.

When I signal to him, he comes over with a duck-like walk. On his face is a mixture of happiness and confusion. In both height and width, he's twice my size. But because he seems so out of place here—it's an aura he radiates—I feel like I'm the big one and he's small.

"How are things in London?" he asks. I was sure that he would say that. "Fine," I answer, "how are things back home?" To my question he responds that things are also fine, and with that it seems that we have concluded the social part of our meeting. I know that he has a lot of time set aside for me, but I have no desire to spend more than half an hour with him.

I don't like him, but it's not his fault. I don't like him because he's the son of a rich building contractor, and because he and his father want to buy the house in Jerusalem.

Even more than I don't like him, I don't like myself. Deep down I'm afraid that I'll agree to sell the house and that it's just a matter of settling on the price.

When he pulls out the sketch of how the property will look after they demolish the house and put up a high-rise, I feel sick. With great enthusiasm, he enumerates the special features of this thirty-story monstrosity. In bright yellow marker, they've outlined the two apartments that they will set aside for me and my brother Amir. We would receive free passes to the health club and pool and be exempt from the not-inconsiderable fees. He makes this last point with raised eyebrows and a half-smile, as if we are now sharing a secret.

In addition to all that—and this he hints to me after my prolonged silence—they are willing to consider paying us some small monetary compensation, but only a small one of course. "Not large at all," he says, looking at me accusingly. As our looks meet, I notice that he has a beautiful face, and that he's completely worn out after delivering his speech.

I'll never be capable of carrying through this type of negotiation. I ask only one question: "What will happen to the well?" He doesn't know what I'm talking about. "There's a well on the site," I explain. He smiles, a little unsure of himself. "Fine, we'll cover it." I ask if it's not possible to preserve it, and he smiles again. No doubt he thinks I'm a little crazy. "We'll have to cover it," he says.

Now I have a week to decide and he has a whole day until his return flight to Israel. For a moment, I consider inviting him back to our place. Steven wouldn't forgive me for it. Also, Kobi Levi doesn't seem like the type who would consider landing in the living room of a male couple the highest form of entertainment. I forget the idea, wish him good luck, and ask for the copy of *Yedi'ot Aharonot* that's sticking out of his bag. He agrees to give it to me, despite the fact that it's clear that reading this Hebrew newspaper is the only thing on his agenda for the day.

On the Underground I read the whole newspaper. It's like a quick visit to Israel—the first few pages of the paper don't make me want to extend this visit, but the middle pages do just that. Reading them I get a sudden rush of nostalgia. Feelings of yearning search me out like secret agents; they find me—and then they attack. I close my eyes and see the house in Jerusalem. I want to convey my feelings to someone—but there is no one.

The Midrash tells us that King David, when he was planning to build the Temple, threw a shard into the well in order to prevent the waters of the deep from rising and flooding Jerusalem. Our family legend has it that that very well was the one in the courtyard of our house in Musrara. And there is more to the story: The stubbornness of my *savta*, Grandma Rachel, about hanging on to life, and hanging on to us by keeping us on a short leash, came from a certainty that after her death the waters of the deep would rise from the well in the courtyard. For she was the only person who knew what shards to throw in the well, where to get them, and what spells and prayers should accompany that magical act.

From the depths of my childhood rise the sounds of the courtyard and of the well in its center: the croaking of the frogs, the riotous noise of the children at play, the sweet sound of my grandmother's singing as she does the laundry—and the voice of my mother, far less sweet, a voice which blends wondrously with that of the frogs. In that mix of sounds, I can also hear the screams from the night that they found the body of my uncle Shmuel floating in the well. I was three years old and didn't understand what was going on, but then neither did anyone else. For years the argument raged as to the cause of that mysterious drowning. Was it a suicide? Was it an act of revenge by one of the underground militias?

But then there wasn't much time to consider the event. Savta Rachel, who seemed immortal, was grief-stricken over the loss of her son and came down with a difficult and demanding illness. Because the family knew that she would never die, they prepared themselves to live with her endless dying until their own deaths.

In addition to her unique relationship to the well, there were two reasons, no less important, that prevented Savta from leaving this world. One was personal and one was national. The first was that her death would precipitate an ugly fight among her three sons over the inheritance. But there never was such a fight. Uncle Shmuel died in the well. Uncle Yosef went to America to get rich—and he did get rich—and lost all interest in us and our property. My parents, modest and without ambition, stayed and lived in the simply furnished house. They had no idea of the stupendously increasing value of the property.

The second reason for Savta's immortality was the fact that our house was the last in the row of houses that faced the border. In the days of the Turks it changed hands often. At times it was in the hands of Arabs and at times in the hands of Jews—until Savta Rachel's grandfather bought it for a lot of money from a sheikh who built a palace for himself in Ramallah. Savta was sure that the struggle over the house wasn't only among its lawful inheritors but between the heirs of Isaac and Ishmael. She was convinced that her death would bring with it the collapse of our powerful hold in Musrara.

In any case, she did die—finally and unambiguously—and left my parents in a crisis of faith from which they never recovered. Their whole lives were shaped by the fact that the family's great matriarch ruled over them and guided them. Now they had to learn the very basic act of making decisions. During my grandmother's life, my parents got along beautifully; her death forced them to confront both the problems of life and each other. Dad began to neglect his accounting office; in the end he took early retirement and became depressed. Mom, on the other hand, became even more compulsive about her volunteer work. In the neighborhood, they would say about her that if someone was sick anywhere in the city she would go out to take care of them, even at the cost of neglecting her own children.

It was not true. Mom found time for Amir, and even for me. I say "even" because I was such a quiet child that I was more often noticed when I was absent than when I was present. Mom followed our every step. In school, in the scouts, she was up-to-date on every detail. She had a way of being present in her look, her touch, in the way she presented a plate of apple slices. She also had the unique ability to find us clothes that grew with us. Like the miracle of the jug of oil, somehow there was always another fold of cloth that would allow her to take out the pants. When its time had come, the old article of clothing was tossed up in the attic, "for the grandchildren." For Mom the grandchildren were a present reality, as if she had met them already and was only waiting for their reappearance. The attic soon became full of things for them—toys, games, clothes, volumes of old children's newspapers.

The person who suffered most from Mom's philanthropy was Dad, who was totally neglected by her. He worked out his frustrations by frequenting the halls of the neighborhood health clinic, where he waited to see a certain Dr. Ashira. Dad appeared daily at her small clinic up the street and reported on his illnesses with his typical precision. I'll never understand how she found the patience for him.

In the end he got disgusted with her, and for two or three weeks he knocked on the door of Dr. Sahar. The elderly doctor told him exactly what he thought of him and his real and imagined diseases. Dad's self-respect didn't allow him to return to Dr. Ashira. Because there were only two doctors on staff at the clinic, he had no choice but to wander around the city, dressed in an old suit that he always thought of as new, and look for the one doctor in existence who would listen to him, believe him, and cure him. That doctor he never found.

While Dad wandered between clinics and pharmacies, Mom made a parallel circuit to visit the many sick people who made up her kingdom. When their circuits converged on Ben Yehuda Street, she completely ignored him—her real patient—and continued on to more distant and more important patients. The sicker they were, the greater her satisfaction.

During the Six-Day War, Mom established a front-line medical center next to Mandelbaum Gate for the wounded. She didn't have the chance to treat even one of the wounded. A Jordanian shell fell on the makeshift tent, killing her and wounding Dr. Sahar, who had volunteered to serve at her side. Thus the joy of victory that accompanied that war eluded us. But for Dad there was one small consolation: the liberation of the Old City enabled us to bury Mom in an excellent spot along the Messiah's future route. Dad devoted the next few years to immortalizing her memory and caring for her grave—which became his favorite place. He spent his last years there, and there too he died—broken-hearted, leaning against Mom's grave. What remained was Amir, me, and the house. We spent a lot of time in the courtyard, spinning out old memories and hosting friends.

I was discharged from the army and had all the time in the world. I was determined not to make any plans and not to assume any responsibilities. Although Amir had reached thirty, he had a similar philosophy. He could be industrious when necessary, but he found no special reason to work: we had plenty of money. Instead he put all of his energy into traveling, holding long conversations deep into the night, and making coffee. In the evenings we would sit in the courtyard, light candles on the edge of the well, and exchange views with guests or occasional tenants.

We always had a friend or two living with us. Either they were between apartments, or it simply was convenient for them. In addition, there were a few couples with no place of their own. They used one of our five bedrooms for their passionate trysts. Until today—our old key is in the pockets of people we hardly know. In fact, a key wasn't necessary; the door was never locked.

The charmed days of the house and its courtyard ended when Amir met a girl from Tel Aviv, Liat, during a trip to the Sinai. He moved in with her in stages—each time with another plastic bag and clothes, until nothing was left in his room. On his rare visits, he told me that Liat didn't want to get married and didn't want children. That didn't bother him. In fact, nothing she did—or didn't do—bothered him. He let her organize his life, a life that became more and more distant from mine.

Alone, without Amir, I wasn't worth much. The friends dwindled. The old furniture raised dust and the courtyard shrank as it was dwarfed by the neighboring houses, which sprouted like shooting plants. In the end I felt that all of this history was too much for me, too heavy, and that I needed something else, something totally different, and distant.

That something was Steven, and I found him in London. We met in an Underground station. When I think about it, I realize that it may not have been as random as it seemed then. He simply waited for me there, as if this was the right station. Each of us was the other's train.

I was happy to discover myself anew, and with somebody. Steven was older, more experienced, and wiser than me. He grew up in a very Christian family. He worked at an uninteresting job in the post office, but his hours were easy, and we had every evening to ourselves—and the night. Especially the night. I lived a full life and was happy each and every minute. A person who has never found himself won't understand what I'm saying.

For over a year I spoke only English, I thought only of London, only of Steven. I pushed away anything that wasn't part of my life there. A postcard from Amir, a postcard to Amir, no more. Steven and I were bound together by more and more ties. We spoke a lot about our future together. We had something in common: we were both trying to cut ourselves free from the past.

For Steven it could have worked. He had nowhere to go back to. When he was a child he was raped by a family member. When he grew up he ran away from home. The few pictures that he had, he had destroyed.

For me, it was more complicated. Steven was the man I wanted, but beneath that desire there were torrents of longing for Israel. In the mornings, shards of dreams surfaced in my consciousness—they were dreams from home. As time passed, my resistance weakened. Getting up in the morning became increasingly difficult. I was a creature from one world who was stuck in another. The charm of British life slowly evaporated. Although I was stubbornly determined to hold on to happiness, I knew that I was only grasping its tail.

When Kobi Levi called from Levi and Sons, Limited, I had already realized that a signal from home was only a matter of time.

I return from the airport, fall into bed, and drop off to sleep immediately.

That night Savta returns, not summoned and not expected. She appears in my dream, insists on putting things in order. She doesn't have to say anything. That she appears, in her bright blue dress, is in itself an explicit announcement. It doesn't matter to her that unlike others in the family I have never believed in dreams. So far as she is concerned, we are all her subjects. When she wants something, nothing can stop her; not even death, which has tried. I can't even think of rebelling.

Steven thinks I'm ill. He asks no questions. We are both familiar with sudden reminders of the past: when such a wave washes over one of us, we put on a bathrobe and go to bed. His robe is nicer than mine, so I wear his.

I escape into sleep, but it's not much of a consolation because Savta darts out from the folds of sleep, this time wearing the red dress. She had only two dresses, blue and red. She looks impatient. I get out of bed and seek refuge in the leather easy chair near the window. And then one night is over, followed by another, and another. Jerusalem returns—as does the house, and friends—and I am overcome with longing and fear.

Savta wants me to return to Israel. I know it. She argues with me without words—with only her facial expressions. Her look is so accusing, and so powerful. I want to tell her no—but I can't.

All at once I see where all of this is leading—like the resolution of a mystery story: I'll have to return home. I'll have to leave Steven behind. Savta will never leave me alone. She'll soon become the most solid presence around me. She—and the house, which I thought I had forgotten. The house will become both my present and my future, like an additional floor in the story of my life.

Kobi Levi is waiting for me at Ben-Gurion airport. I don't know how he knew that I was flying in, but he is there. He is carrying new plans for the high-rise. He has sunglasses perched on his head, even though it is dark outside. In the plans the tower looks quite different now, and we are allotted four apartments—two for Amir and two for me. As for the monetary compensation, it too has grown—considerably, in fact. He tells me this with great force, with dedication, looking me straight in the eye. Let's be straight, he says. You have no idea how much this land is now worth; they are building hotels and office towers there. There is no doubt that you are selling an excellent piece of real estate. "Excellent" sounds like something with gravy when he says it—maybe steak.

And then comes the surprise. He rolls out another blueprint from his bag. On it, in attractive colors, is a sketch of the house's courtyard with the well at its center. They have made it look like an amphitheater, with steps all around, like the compound in front of the Damascus Gate. He understands who he is dealing with and has planned everything around the well, as if the lovely high-rise were rising from it. But Savta, who is seeing him from within me, is smarter, or at least more ancient. She knows that it's either the tower or the well. In truth, they can't both exist.

Don't mess around with Savta—that's what I'm thinking as Kobi Levi rolls out his plans with a victorious gesture. She can knock down your lovely tower and send it down into the deep.

We get up to shake hands, and I say that it doesn't seem that it will work at present. Maybe a little later. That's as close to "no" as I can get.

He follows me until the exit from the terminal and I tell him that I've got to rest, I can't discuss it now. When he leaves me, I sneak back in and check myself out in the bathroom: I'm sweating, out of breath, but alive.

Savta and I get closer to each other. If she is going to stick so close to me, I might as well make my peace with her and stop fighting. She is perched at the threshold of my consciousness: watchful, making astute observations but not interfering. We have long conversations. I love her company. Sooner or later we will have to confront each other on the big issue. From where she sits, she can't help but see the whole picture of my life, including Steven.

He's there—and not there. We talk on the phone, write to each other, and mostly, we think about each other. There is no chance that he will live here, I know it. But he's part of my life.

The return to the house is easier than I thought. In the first week, I do nothing but clean up. The process slowly uncovers the floors, the furniture, and the memories that are in every room—and it uncovers me, the person that I was, and now am. At times I stop working and sit near the well and listen, and think. The old rhythm returns; day turns to night. When the church bells ring at midnight, I get up and go to sleep in my bed. Just like back then. I stare into the darkness through the arched window in my room. Even this very specific darkness is familiar to me.

Savta thinks it unhealthy that I'm not working. She used to get up early every morning—I remember it well—and didn't rest for a moment during the day. She doesn't quite understand this "thinking" of mine. Is there really so much to think about? We cook together. Her old recipes come to life. There's no doubt that her delicate cooking is better than the British food that I learned to cook in my class. But it's because of that course that I can cook at all.

The aromas of home cooking attract friends, as in the old days. Amir too visits at times. He says, "It's a pity to see this big old house go to waste like this. If only we could use it for something good, so people could enjoy its beauty."

Savta listens and nods her head.

"Thinking of something specific?" I ask. Savta, from her place in the window sill, her thumbs and her index finger under her chin, seems pensive. She is faster than both of us. She always had creative ideas.

"A restaurant," she says.

"A restaurant," he says.

We both walk through the rooms and discover that the house and the courtyard were destined for that purpose. The largest room declares its function—the main dining area of a restaurant. The two small rooms to the side are appropriate for small groups in each; and Dad's large old study for the kitchen. We also have a name, almost self-evident: "The Well."

And now the house is buzzing again. And again we see friends and friends of friends, and again the smells of Savta's cooking waft through the halls. Amir and Liat drive up every evening from Tel Aviv. For the first week he is the barman, I'm the cook, Liat is the waitress. In the second week we already have three waiters, and another barman, another cook, and a dishwasher. Every day after midnight we sit around the well, like we used to. We are surrounded by the last of the diners, illuminated by the colorful lighting we put up, and talk. Amir and I make Savta's special pine nut tea and serve it to everyone.

It takes me a while to understand that if Amir knows how to prepare Savta's secret tea—which even my mother didn't know how to make—it's a sign that she is somehow with him, too. I confront him with this realization and he confirms it—with some degree of embarrassment. He says this happens to him only when he comes back to the house in Musrara, and he admits that is the reason that he returns.

It's night already. We are both a little drunk, and we speak openly about Savta. We have a complicated relationship with her, of course. Amir contends that I'm crazy. I tell him that I'm fine—he's the crazy one. We argue for a long time and we both have excellent arguments. In the end we both succeed in convincing the other.

The eve of Yom Kippur is the first day I have off in almost a year. I visit my parents' graves on the Mount of Olives. The gravestones have aged very quickly. It seems as if Amir has never been here and if he has, he never left a sign of his visit. But Mom and Dad are happy here, I'm sure: they are now closer to each other than they ever were during their lives.

After I weed the grass around the graves, I sit down to rest, leaning against Mom's gravestone and looking out over the Old City. It's not that I'm having a religious experience, but feelings arise—and I don't know what to call them. The air here seems fuller, sweeter, richer than anywhere else. I could stay here for a few years and not eat: this air is so nourishing. An old gravedigger is working up the slope. Sounds from the old city rise up. Since Dad's funeral, I haven't been in a cemetery, and now, for the first time, I discover how pleasant it is here. The best ties are the ones with the dead.

I'm still thinking about that when I hear Savta's voice from deep within me, a voice that is hoarse, rich, and sweet, and she tells me to look at the graves of her grandmother and grandfather, her brothers and her sister and her other sister, her many cousins, their kids, grandchildren and great-grandchildren. She also wants great-grandchildren—and great-great-grandchildren. And of course I'm not going to supply them. This section of earth will be empty of the graves of my descendants. I will be the last grave.

Her need for the line to continue is so powerful that I can feel it burning in me. But her need, as justified as it is, is not my need. I'm different, completely different. I look deep within myself—and within her—and say, soundly, completely and absolutely—No.

At night, in the pleasant loneliness of the old house's courtyard, I tie a rope to the metal pipe next to the well, take my clothes off, and let myself down into the well.

The water is very, very cold. I go down and up, down and up, until it is no longer so cold. It was Savta who once gave me that idea. She had a kind of saying: only one who was very familiar with the depths really knew life. I look up and see the slice of sky defined by the edges of the well—with its own set of stars. When I was a child, I thought that these stars were our own private stars and that someday I would inherit them. And now I think that that someday is right now—tonight.

The Sol Popovitch War

Translated by Michael Weingrad

After her military service, my niece did exactly what every other Israeli her age does: she traveled as far away from Israel as she could for the least amount of money. When she returned, she had a bagful of stories to tell. Some of them I forgot soon after she told them; the others I forgot later. But I can't get one story out of my mind.

It was in the middle of her trip. They were camped out on some beach on the far edge of India. At the end of the beach there was a guesthouse, and when you passed it and went a little farther, you came to a bar. At three in the morning, when everyone else was already stoned, she met an Israeli there, about sixty years old. Not that it was a big surprise to meet another Israeli in India, even one so much older than the usual backpackers. But he was different, as if a distant wind had brought him there. She was curious about him, and it didn't take much to get him talking. When she heard his story, told with a kind of sad complacency, she couldn't help but believe every word.

Even though the story is not my own, I want to relay it here exactly as I heard it.

My name is Ephraim Zusman. That won't mean a thing to you, you're too young. But I was once a journalist. I used to publish articles in the Israeli press on military and security matters. I never worked for just one newspaper. Maybe I didn't want to be obligated, and maybe none of them wanted me because they were afraid of my independence. This was during the period when journalists still took care not to irritate the government. I had excellent sources, and I wasn't letting anyone scare me. This is an advantage, but no one thought so then. I had principles. I would never agree to cuts in my reports. I would write at length, giving explanations, analysis. In short, I tangled with a lot of editors. But in the army they appreciated me, also in the secret services. They knew that I wasn't just in a hurry to make headlines.

Unfortunately, despite all that, I couldn't make ends meet. My mother had a very large inheritance from her parents, who once owned a porcelain store in Antwerp, and she gave me half of the interest it generated each month. She believed in me and thought that, even if it took time, ultimately people would understand how great I was.

At some stage of the game, I started to feel that the time had come to hang my hat somewhere. That maybe one big story could land me a real job and a comfortable salary. And just when I started thinking that way, I felt something tug on the end of my line. Something big.

Even now I can't reveal to you the source for my story. He himself denied the whole thing afterward, especially when he saw the consequences. I already had the story, which is what counts.

It began, as these things always do, in a random enough way. I was asked to meet with a senior officer for a general briefing. He was someone I had known for many years, and who enjoyed meeting with me more than I did with him. You know, there are always those types who feel really important when journalists are speaking with them. This guy, who had once been high up in intelligence, had recently been pushed to the side, so he never had anything important to tell me. I was a bit surprised then, when they told me that the meeting had to be postponed. It was hard for me to imagine that he had anything urgent enough going on to require that.

When we met a week later, he apologized that he hadn't been able to see me and explained that they had forced some important guest on him. I asked who, and he said, "Just some American." He didn't want to reveal who. Now, believe me, I usually knew who was visiting the army. I would check up on it. A visit from someone from another country could lead to all sorts of things, like strategic pacts, arms sales, that kind of thing. More than once I had landed a good story from something I sniffed out in a minor visit. It seemed suspicious to me that this officer didn't want to tell me who the visitor was. It didn't seem like him. This was someone who really liked to talk. So I figured I had something here.

I started to check it out. I assumed that it wasn't an American but someone from China or Eastern Europe. I had my reasons for looking in these directions; there were a few things cooking then. But I didn't find a thing. No one knew what I was talking about. In the end, I found out that there was only one guest who had visited the army that week, and he was in fact an American. Without hoping for much, I asked a clerk I had befriended in the chief of staff's office if her boss had met with a visitor from abroad that week. Luck smiled on me. She whispered that Sol Popovitch had been in the country, and immediately afterward she regretted having told me.

That wasn't enough, but neither she nor anyone else was ready to reveal anything more. I would say "Sol Popovitch," and the person I was speaking to suddenly became hard of hearing. It was curious. People who told me the most classified things didn't want to talk about the subject, even off the record.

I rang up a friend in Washington who was a long-time military correspondent at ABC. He had no idea who Sol Popovitch was. I gathered that this guy was no senior official in the military or CIA. The correspondent suggested that the name was an alias, that it would be worth checking into further from my side. I would have loved to, but no one here would talk to me about it. I began to lose hope.

A week later, the same friend called me at four in the morning to tell me about a strange coincidence: he had come across the name Sol Popovitch in the financial section of the *Washington Post*. They wrote that he was building a large brewery near Seattle. I assumed that there was no connection to the person who had visited Israel, but I asked him to check the archives anyway. It turned out that there was in fact a Sol Popovitch from Richmond, Virginia, that he was Jewish and very wealthy, and he had been in the brewing industry for many years. Among Jews he was considered rather right-wing. My instincts, which generally are reliable in these matters, began to tell me I might be onto something.

Once again I made my rounds of the General Headquarters and Secret Service. And again no one wanted to tell me anything. There were some who had no inkling of what I was talking about, and others who knew and didn't want to talk. I could feel it. I was pulling my hair out: what could be so top secret about some millionaire from Virginia visiting the army?

Then my source turned up. It was someone I knew on a superficial level, who I had met once at the northern command. We had shaken hands and that was all. He heard from someone that I was interested in this business, and he decided to give me the details. He said that he had to get it off his chest and made me swear never to reveal that it was from him.

And this is the story:

Solomon Popovitch was a long-time donor to the UJA, who had already engraved his name on two or three small forests in Israel, as well as on the youth center in Afula, and on ten ambulances of Magen David Adom, the Israeli Red Cross. But he wanted more. He felt he had something to contribute to the Jewish people, and it wasn't just money. He had close relationships with half of the government; you know how it is with these people. Beyond that, he was a hypochondriac, and because of the twenty rare diseases he was afflicted with, he was convinced that he didn't have many years to live. He had a ton of money, and he was as insistent on giving to Israel as he was on not leaving a cent to his son, his only child. I was never successful in finding out exactly what the story was between the two of them.

They tried to interest Popovitch in all sorts of projects. Mayor Teddy Kollek tried hard to sell him on funding the Jerusalem promenade, but when they took him to see the site he was struck by the fact that it looked out on more Arabs than Jews, so Teddy gave up and went to Sherover for the money. Afterward they ran after him about the museum to commemorate the soldiers of Israel's wars. It was then that they started having him meet with people from the military world. He showed a lot of interest, and they took him to the tank museum, famous battlefields, and so on. They say he cried every time they told him about fallen soldiers. It was clear he was going to give a lot of money, but he wouldn't commit himself to anything. Prime Minister Rabin pushed the military chief of staff into getting personally involved, saying that if they could take him on one really exciting patrol he would get down to business. It seems that there was good chemistry between the general and Popovitch, and the general, in order to make him feel like he was part of the action, told him about some missions that the army was involved in just then, and also took him to visit an air force base.

Everyone almost flipped when Popovitch suggested that he would contribute the money if they named a base after him. It had never happened that a base was named after someone not from the army. They told him this clearly enough. And since he wasn't used to hearing no, he became insulted. He said he didn't see why the State of Israel would be so happy to name a museum for dead soldiers after him, but wouldn't want to honor him with a base of living soldiers. And like a good businessman, he now added a touch of drama: first, he raised the sum, which already stood at many millions of dollars. Second, he canceled the rest of the visit and returned that day to the United States. At the airport he hinted that he wasn't sure that he would come back again since his days were numbered.

The cuts in the military budget were large. Naturally everyone said that it wasn't proper to name an air force base after Sol Popovitch. On the other hand, some thought that it was necessary to find creative solutions, that perhaps they could promise him something and then find a way to get out of it afterward. It was actually an air force commander who was the first to move in the direction of a compromise: he suggested putting a plaque on one of the hangars that would commemorate Sol Popovitch as a friend of the armed forces, and presenting it to him as if the whole squadron were named after him. In the air force they really hoped that this would tip the scales and give them the means to buy the new fleet they wanted. Of course, once they began the negotiations there was no turning back. Popovitch was a lot sharper than the military attaché in Washington who was sent to Virginia to negotiate. He wanted them to put his name not on one hangar but on each of the planes in the squadron, exactly like on the ambulances.

The generals held a closed meeting about this. They were afraid of setting a precedent, but they didn't want to give up the money. The commander of the armored divisions suggested naming a small camp in the Sinai after him, since they were going to return the Sinai to Egypt in any case. The financial advisor to the chief of staff came up with an idea that seemed more promising: instead of naming something tangible after him, like a tank or a cruiser or a base, they would take some abstract concept, like a five-year plan. Let's say the Sol Popovitch one-day field exercises. His name would be on some manila folder, and apart from the donor no one would have to know about it.

Sol Popovitch returned to Israel one last time, to continue the negotiations. It had become the most important thing in his life. He seemed healthy enough, but he assured the chief of staff that his prognosis was worse than ever. In his meeting with the defense minister, he rejected all the proposals they brought to him. The minister tried to move in a new direction: why not some new building at the headquarters of the secret service? In any case the secret service is a civilian body, which makes things less complicated. Popovitch got excited. They had almost closed the deal when he remembered that if the building would be in such a secret place, then no one would know about it or see it. On the other hand, he liked the idea of the secret service. He wanted them to name something operational after him. And then he made a scene with nausea and stomach pains and was rushed off to the Hilton hotel for the night.

My source said that when the donor left, the defense minister and four senior officers sat around the table, exhausted, and began to make jokes about the whole affair. The head of the secret service, who had been called to the meeting, said that if they gave him the money and the manpower, he would be ready to name some minor assassination "Operation Popovitch." Why a minor liquidation, asked the chief of staff, why not a major retaliation? And so, from a joke, things developed until they reached a decision: they would name a war after him.

The next day they sat with him in his hotel suite and told him that if he was really talking about a billion dollars, as sources close to him had indicated, then they would name a war in his honor. He was moved to tears, and the atmosphere became thick with emotion. They drew up a price list for all the wars, starting with the Yom Kippur War, which would go for a song, to the Six-Day War, for which they wanted a billion and a quarter. He said the offer was an attractive one, and money was no object, but he had a lot of reservations about the tactics employed in the various wars (he was unbelievably well informed), and if he was going to lay out so much money he wanted to have a say. So it was decided to name the *next* war for him—it was, after all, still an open question how it would be conducted. They promised to include him in the planning if his health permitted. He assured them that he would hold on until victory, even if it cost him another few years of life.

When the army realized that I knew the whole story and was even going to publish it, they began to conspire against me. First they tried using all the Zionist rhetoric that was in currency then. They said that I would be harming a major donor, and the interests of the state, and the whole sacred concept of the next war. I had no intention of giving up, but when I brought the story to the newspaper I discovered that men in dark sunglasses had already paid a visit to the editor, and they warned him that my story was unreliable and so was I. They told him that I was mentally unstable. I made the rounds of all the newspapers, but no one wanted to hear my voice. I found out that I was completely on my own. It destroyed my entire career. After that they wouldn't take anything from me, and I didn't want to write anymore: if no one wanted to hear the full, exclusive story about the next war, then what could I expect from journalism? Or from Israel?

According to what my niece told me, Ephraim Zusman was carrying with him a file with photographs and other evidence. Whether because of him or because of the constraints of coalition politics, that next war was postponed, and replaced with an entirely different war, and anyway, Popovitch lost his fortune in the economic crisis that hit America soon after the episode. Zusman claims that although Popovitch's health has not improved, he lives pretty well on his estate in southern Virginia, hoping for the best.

Green Island

Translated by Terri Klein

There was a guy who adopted a traffic island. He planted a nice garden with red and blue flowers, small bushes, and a little bit of grass. He did it because he lived in a gloomy apartment: no balcony, no courtyard, nothing at all. It's not that he was such a daring person; he did it because he just wanted a garden.

For almost a year he had a good time. It was so much fun to climb into overalls and work in that garden! It annoyed him that there were people who thought he was crazy—or worse, a sucker—volunteering to do an act of public service. But he was having such a great time, it was all worthwhile.

Until they found out about it. They came from the municipal department of civic works to ask just what he thought he was doing there. Somebody must have ratted on him; otherwise they would never have noticed. He apologized, explained, claimed he really made things better for everyone, but nothing helped. They said that if they caught him gardening on the traffic island again—well, if he didn't cut it out, they would cut it down. And within a week they covered the whole thing with asphalt and painted the asphalt green. End of story.

On Reserve

Translated by Michael Weingrad

I n the army, a story went around among us about Sgt. Eyni.
Once, during training, he went out to look for a water tank
that had been forgotten in the field. When he found it, he
marked it on a map so he could return to the place and get it.
He continued on his way but couldn't locate the battalion.
Suddenly he saw another water tank, and put another dot
on the map—two kilometers from the first—and continued
driving. He saw yet another tank. He drew yet another dot.
This one was three kilometers from the last. So he went on
until he found, let's say, five tanks. Meanwhile it got dark
and he hadn't found the battalion. He called for them to
come get him from the field.

The next day the logistics company commander sent
five trucks to tow back all the water tanks, but they only
found one, and not at the spot where it was marked on the
map. It turned out that Eyni, who didn't know how to navigate, drove around and around in circles and marked the
same water tank five times.

Sgt. Eyni was a real person, but I can't vouch for the story.

And there was a story about a guy who got special leave
when he told his commanding officer that the weekend

before he got laid for the first time, and it was so good that he had to get out again.

That story is true, and I was the commanding officer. It happened a short time after my arrival at the battalion. During my two years there, I heard the story told in many different versions and variations, sometimes adorned with other characters, and maybe it's even still going around the battalion today—the story and its optimistic moral: with the right combination of a mischievous soldier, a good story, and an understanding officer, the impossible becomes possible. Even a weekend leave.

Why I let myself be persuaded then, I'll never know. Maybe it was a weekend that I had the authority to give leave to someone, and the first one with a good story got it. Or maybe his passion touched me, and reminded me of what I went through myself with Sarit during almost all of my army service—those maddening intervals between distant weekends.

I'm one of those people who no one expected to leave the army; they said I was addicted. They laughed at me when I signed up for another six months. They said, why run to sign up every half a year? Sign up once for all nine years and get it over with.

There were even moments when I considered doing it. When your soldiers look at you like you're God, and your superiors slap you on the back, and you feel responsible for the fate of the country—or at least for the northern border—and finally the corps commander himself arrives at your platoon in a helicopter to grace you with his presence, making you feel like you're the best thing that's happened to the Jewish people since Bar Kokhba, and then invites you to join the standing army and right away travel abroad for advanced studies—well, it's tempting.

And there's also the atmosphere. You sit with the guys on recon as if at a campfire, huddling together around the flickering lights of the communications equipment, telling stories. You see everybody covered in dust, just like you, and the most important thing in the world is always about to happen any minute—whether joint maneuvers, or training, or operations in Lebanon—and you start to love it a little.

I got out because I wanted to marry Sarit, and I promised her I'd be a full-time husband, not some hero who comes home once a month and disappears into his own fame. And I wanted to study at the Technion, because I felt that I could be something more than a professional soldier.

But Sarit was finished with me before I finished the army. And the Technion didn't accept me. I was so sure of myself then that I hadn't applied to any other programs. The next year I applied to the top three universities in Israel and got accepted by all of them.

Being released from the army was hugely depressing— not because of Sarit and not because of the Technion. It's that emptiness, when there are no exercises or maneuvers to prepare for, when no one needs you on the double, when you feel lower than low and suddenly your mother is the central figure in your life again. I know a lot of people who have fallen into depression after being released from the army, but I don't know a single one who admits it.

I spent a year trying out ten different jobs. I rented a studio apartment in Rehovot. I screwed around like a wild man. I got wasted every way possible. I insisted I was happy, but I felt used up and miserable.

Until Sarit called me and we met. At first just to see each other. But after two or three times we decided to try again, and the trial period ended in a marriage and three wonderful children. The oldest, Amir, is already eighteen. Meanwhile, I finished my studies in electrical engineering and started work at the Mekhlafim Co., and little by little I got ahead in life. While serving periodically on reserve duty, of course.

Reserve duty.

At first it was hard. You come in like a big shot from the regular army, only everyone around you is thirty or forty years old, veterans from all the wars, and they remind you you're a kid. When you give them an order they look at you slantwise.

And, idiot that I am, I met them head-on. The yelling, the scolding, and taking everything too much to heart. I'm a hard-headed person—call of duty, security of the region, and all that jazz.

It took me a year or two to get away from that and into the mind-set of being in the reserves: everything in good time. We're older, after all, no need to run around breaking our backs, and I even took on that slantwise look, and soon used it better than the others. Like when I took aside the operations officers who came to check our combat readiness, and I cut them off with that look. I sat them facing the border, and told them that we had fought here "in the Six" (Day War, of course), and that they had nothing to worry about. After five years I was made battalion deputy commander.

Being a deputy commander puts you through the mill. Running all the time to briefings and intelligence updates and border assessments. I was at reserve duty more than I was at work. Sarit said, take control of your life; now you're volunteering to do what you wouldn't do for money when you were in the regular army. I made it through because in the reserves, just as in the regular army, there are good guys, and the only really important thing is getting the job done and not some stupid instructions laid down by bureaucrats who don't carry a rifle. And so it's not necessary to run to every division training seminar (even if the brigade commander himself explains to you on the phone that it's vital), or even to be on every sector patrol in Lebanon. Otherwise, life isn't life, it's just being on reserve.

I began to love the reserves. I noticed there were others like me. Men who prefer to be on reserve duty, to get out in the air a bit, to struggle with a different range of problems, to go back and become what they were ten, twenty years ago: young men, sure of themselves, surrounded by their buddies, fighting for a just cause (most of the time).

And another reason to love the reserves snuck up on me. One time I had to be at the storage facility in the north at seven in the morning. I meant to leave the night before and sleep over in Naharia at the home of a friend from the battalion, but I didn't remember to phone him until the last minute, and he wasn't in.

I went to Naharia anyway. I spent the night in a hotel by the sea, and suddenly I found myself alone, wandering in a strange city, something I hadn't done in years, looking at the other people living their lives under the shade of the trees by the deep-green sea, far-off and calm. I sat on a bench and felt relaxed, removed from the constant tension that always surrounds me. Just being a man on a bench, not a father, not a head engineer, not a husband, not a battalion deputy commander. And I had a great time like that, being there with myself. So I made it a tradition to travel to Naharia a couple of times a year on the evening before reserve duty, my only vacation from being eternally on alert.

The second or third time—always in that hotel, always on that bench—I treated myself to a cup of coffee and a piece of cake, which were both out of this world, as if they had been made from ingredients that don't exist in Tel Aviv. I told myself, you see, you're living your life right. Everything is in place. You have everything you want, as good as it gets, the best kids and the kindest wife and a good job and everything. My blessings stretched from Naharia to Cyprus. And I was ready to get to sleep, because it was late and I had to be up at six in the morning. We were about to begin reserve duty in the eastern sector of Lebanon, and I wanted to get started on the right foot. Also they were already closing the café (Naharia, with all of its charms, shuts down rather early), and yet I still wandered a little, here and there, there and here, and then . . .

Then in front of me stood a U.N. soldier, a black guy, solid, and he smiled at me, and we stood there some two or three minutes and didn't say a word. We just stared into each other's eyes, as if we were playing a game to see who would blink first. But no one gave in. And then he said, come.

He led me to my hotel. The clerk at the reception desk looked at us a little strangely, but I didn't care. It turned out that this soldier had a room on the floor below mine. We went there. From the window you could see the sea lit up in the moon's silver light. When he undressed, his dark body was bathed in this light, which brought out its every detail against the pale background of the wall. I jumped into bed with him without any surprise or hesitation, as if I had been with men my whole life, and for all his strength and stamina

I wore him out after half a night of lovemaking, when he fell asleep while we were doing it, his legs on the pillow, his head against the window, smiling at the fading moon.

We had the shittiest reserve duty ever, and I forgot about everything that happened. Two of our soldiers were wounded, and we had to deal with the civilian population on the one hand and ambushes on the other, and then there was a whole platoon talking about refusing to serve. The whole time I found myself arguing politics, which is my weakest suit. And the worst was that at the end the battalion commander called me to tell me he was going to Canada for two years and asked me to "mind the store." Without wanting to (and mainly without having any alternative), I took over the battalion.

Like that time in the reserves, the year afterward was crazy. My father died suddenly of a heart attack. A few months later, Sarit's mother was diagnosed with cancer. Sarit herself had severe back problems and was running from doctor to doctor. And all this exactly when my work-place, Mekhlafim, began to go downhill along with the other union-run companies. There was also a lot of pressure then in the reserves, and they called us to Lebanon once more that year, this time in the western sector.

I was the battalion commander, with wave after wave of soldiers coming to see me—this one whose mother is sick, and that one with the pregnant wife, and a third on proba-tion for refusing to serve. Everyone on my back, plus the brigade commander who needs me every time they call him from general headquarters.

So I did what anyone would have done in my case: I put the episode with the U.N. soldier into the safe in my head and locked it, saying, it was an accident, something like that happens to everyone once in his life without it leading to anything else.

Only when I arrived in Naharia again, the evening before reserve duty, suddenly the episode came back to me. I sat on my bench, but I didn't feel any peace or quiet or happiness or anything, only the guilt and shock I had buried for eight months. In particular I thought about Sarit. How could I do a thing like that to her, when all my life it's been clear to me that I'm not like the other guys in the reserves, who brag about fucking around on the side. I didn't even have the comforting possibility that comes with any other betrayal—that is, to tell her and ask forgiveness. Right, go and tell your wife that you slept with some guy, a U.N. soldier, on the way to reserve duty.

After a few hours, when I calmed down a little bit, I went for a walk on the beach. I watched a girl on her tricycle and a man with a dark hat tilted over his freckled nose, accompanied by his dog. That's how I wandered around until it was already late. I walked once more up the beach and then turned down along the river, and then . . .

Then, in almost the same place as the U.N. solider, there stood a young guy in a black jersey and shorts—I don't know why he wasn't cold, since it was February—and he looked at me with serious, blue eyes. He had very short hair with just one black lock that spiraled down between those sky-colored eyes. I walked up to him and stopped with my thumbs tucked in my belt. I felt that as I stood there, like an officer on military inspection, the wind was leaving my sails, and that I immediately had to make the toughest decision, much more difficult than anything in the army. All right, then, I said to myself. And to him I said, let's go.

Right after reserve duty it was time for my yearly vacation. We went to the new King Solomon Hotel in Eilat and enjoyed everything, at a safe distance from our three good children and from my three hundred soldiers, some of whom were already looking for me to help them get out of the next term of service.

Every day over breakfast, I looked at Sarit and thought to myself, how, how is it that I stumbled like that in Naharia (and twice!). Suddenly I had all the time in the world to feel guilty, to ask myself all the questions: what's missing for you with this wonderful woman, and why men all of a sudden, and how could it happen twice? Toward the end of the vacation, new and even more dangerous questions arose, such as, what if this is really what you want?

But I didn't let these questions get to me. I returned to work and to life, and also to two days of hectic training at the reserve installation on the coastal plain. There they informed me that Eli, the battalion commander, wasn't coming back from Canada. I said to myself, being battalion commander wouldn't be so terrible; anyway, all the responsibility has always been on my shoulders. That evening the brigade commander added another "falafel" star to my rank, and two hundred men showered me with water and praises, and Doron the platoon leader became my deputy commander, and the brigade commander said that if there was any company he could count on it was us.

The questions, frightening as they were, also became part of the routine. I even found myself beginning to enjoy it a little—like an actor, perhaps: that I had more than one identity, that there was a dark corner in my life where I could throw off all conventions, where I was anonymous, just an attractive man.

And so it became a regular thing. The day before reserves I would go to Naharia. An hour or two before sundown I would enjoy the blessed peace and quiet that came to me there. I would eat a good dinner while the colors were at their most magical, drink a cup of coffee, and go right to the same spot. I soon understood that guys like that were drawn there. And there was always someone, as if he had been sent to wait just for me. Almost without speaking, we would go to my hotel and let loose with all our strength.

None of the things that made me anxious ever happened. I didn't meet anyone I knew, I wasn't asked too many questions, and I wasn't beaten or robbed. I merely accumulated a trove of experiences with people, most of whose names I didn't know, and certainly not their real names. I didn't try to explain myself to myself, I only understood that this was me, with my wild little secret, cut off from everything else.

And in the hurly-burly of reserve duty, I could always forget it and concentrate on ammunition and ambushes and wounded soldiers and evaluations—the whole gamut of things the army throws at you. And over the years I established myself in the battalion and the brigade, and they even talked with me about returning to the regular army.

Looking into the wise and gentle eyes of Sarit, who never cast doubts or asked questions, I said in my mind what I couldn't say aloud. Forgive me, my innocent Sarit, I'm a sinful person and I'm not worth your little finger. And I thought, maybe this is the price we must pay for all the good that has befallen us in life. And I loved her even more.

Last year we did reserve duty for the first time during the Intifada. From the vibes I got during the briefings, I knew there would be trouble. Even men who never cause problems were suddenly coming at me with stories, and not only because of politics but just because of a bad feeling in the gut, a desire not to mix rifles with women and children, or whatever you want to call it. When I went out on the first day, I also felt wooden and grimy, as if the ambivalence of all the soldiers was gathered up in me. And suddenly I also wanted to have someone to go to and tell the truth: I'm not up for this, I don't want to go there.

The day before reserves, in midsummer, I even wanted to steer clear of Naharia and find comfort in Sarit's arms instead, but the urge attacked me and became urgent.

I have to confess that in the meantime I began to understand that there really is something about men that turns me on, and I noticed where my eyes wander in the street and where they stop. And without turning this into some big philosophy of life, I summed it up this way: guys turn you on. So what? Everyone's bisexual, only no one talks about it.

I traveled to Naharia.

No one was there. Just when I really wanted it. I went up and down the length of the beach, I combed all the streets, and I returned to the spot on the bank of the dry riverbed, and I saw a couple stepping into an alley, where they disappeared, so much in love, and also a few stars looking for the moon that wasn't there, and there wasn't a guy anywhere. And it was already late.

I went to the hotel and stood by the window. The beach was dark. I got undressed, closed my eyes, and tried to fall asleep, without success. I wanted to fantasize about the times before but I couldn't. I tried to avoid the big questions, but my head wouldn't let me. The harder I closed my eyes, and tried to order myself to enter the narrow passage into sleep—the more my wakefulness increased and random thoughts forced their way into my head.

I got dressed and went down to the street. Dead silence. I walked slowly to the next street corner, aware of every movement of my muscles. I crossed the alley and continued on, and then sat on the curb and remembered how I used to play street ball when I was a boy, and nothing came into my head in any proper order, just chaos and a big confusion of images. I didn't notice that someone was by my side until I suddenly heard, "Shalom." I lifted my head and saw a soldier, in a uniform that looked like it had just been ironed, smiling with an alert expression and asymmetrical dimples and bright eyes. I was so startled I was speechless. I looked up, and he said, "What's your name?" and I told him. Not like usual when I would give a false name—each time a different one—this time I said my name.

His name was Eytan.

We strolled through the darkness, talking about this and that, where he was from, where I'm from. I wasn't even sure what he wanted. Maybe he had something entirely different in mind. But he was lovely, just lovely, young but mature, with a fantastic smile between those dimples of his, which flashed in the darkness with a pure brilliance. And I said to myself, if this guy goes to bed with me, it will be the most beautiful thing in the world.

Though this thought was needling me the whole time, like a bee buzzing around my head just to torment me, I was afraid even to hope. And besides, there was a person here, not just a body, and he had a brain, and we were talking. This was different than the men who shared a moment's pleasure with me, and spoke a couple of sentences or less.

And perhaps the fear already snuck in that this time it was something more.

In the end, we stood beneath a dim streetlamp like a couple of embarrassed high school kids, and he asked if we could meet again. My heart was pounding. My head swam. I wanted nothing more than to touch him.

I didn't want to ruin the moment and say the wrong thing. I said, yes, sure we could meet again. I asked if we could exchange numbers. He said yes, but that I would have to be careful when I called. That was the one thing that really confirmed it, since up till then it all might have been a misunderstanding, maybe some meeting with a lost boy looking for a connection to the world. But the moment he asked me to be discrete we were both on the same wavelength, and it was probably the only thing I had learned at that point about the lives of that kind of men. It's like you join a secret club, an underground, and there are definite rules about secrecy, lines you don't cross and that sort of thing.

I wrote my work number on the back of a receipt that I tore in half. He wrote his on the other half, in a schoolboy's loops, and he looked at me with an expression of both hope and a little sadness—maybe sad at the expected parting. I remembered to mention that I was headed for reserve duty, and he asked when, and I said tomorrow, and I looked at my watch and laughed, saying, today, actually, in a little while. And then he blurted out, "Call me after reserve duty," and he kissed me on the lips, turned around, and left.

I stood there, staring at him as he walked away and disappeared into a night without a moon.

I felt like I had my own Intifada inside me as I went off to deal with the real thing. This time there were even more troubles than in Lebanon. One platoon commander was out of the country, another was sick, and Doron, who had his own serious problems at work, wasn't much help. Meanwhile, I functioned as if I was dreaming, not all there. Every few hours, I took out the piece of paper with Eytan's phone number, even though I already knew it by heart. I tried to recall the details of his face but I couldn't. I only conjured up the dimples, even starker the further he was away. When the officers gave me their reports on the rocks and the barricades and the patrols, those dimples came back to me and I wanted to run away from everything, especially from myself.

When I called home, I felt a new heaviness over the line. The orders left my mouth in a jumble and there were moments when I thought I wasn't going to make it. I don't know how things came out all right. Not that we did exemplary service, there in the rock-strewn alleys of the strange city. But we did what was necessary and we got out of there without causing injuries or being injured—at least not visible ones.

From time to time I picked up the telephone, dialed the northern prefix, another number or two, and then put down the receiver. I felt that in a terrible way something beautiful was happening to me: I was falling in love with a guy.

As if everything that happened before him had been nothing more than a thrill, a complicated pleasure, but nothing serious. Something between myself and—myself. For really, what did I have with those men in Naharia? What part of myself did I leave them with? And then here's this guy I can't get out of my head. Just like that, all of a sudden.

One evening when reserve duty was over, I was sitting at my mother's with Sarit and the kids. As everyone was caught up in some TV show, I looked at my mom's face, wrinkled behind the thick lenses of her glasses. Suddenly I wanted to start crying, put my head on her shoulder, and ask, how is it that sometimes there aren't any solutions? Why didn't my straight and narrow path prepare me for some things? I, who spent my whole life solving everyone else's problems, now have a huge problem of my own and I don't know where to turn.

I looked up at the wall, at the photo of my father from the War of Independence, with his khaki shirt and his World War II rifle. I tried to imagine what my father would say about a problem like this, if it could be presented in a completely abstract way.

My father had two favorite sayings that were as contradictory as he was. He would say that there's no such thing as a problem without a solution; and also that when there's a problem without a solution, let life offer its own solutions.

The next day I called Eytan. His mother answered in a clear voice. "Eytan is in the army." Of course. I left my phone number, at home and at work, resolutely fending off her questions.

Eytan called at work. He was at an educational seminar.

Entirely aware of the danger, I took off from the office early, leaving a message that I was out on business and would be back later, and drove to Netanya. Eytan was waiting for me on the sidewalk by the base, just as nervous as I was. He got into the car and stared ahead, at the road.

We drove north a bit, then took a side road along the sea, which was churning with foam and uniformly gray. In the distance some boys from the nearby immigration center were hanging out. My palm rested on the knob of the stick shift as my gaze sank deep into the sea, and I breathed in the hot, salty air until I felt, to my relief, his hand slide tentatively over mine. Without speaking we listened to the gulls.

Three times in my life I've fallen in love. The first time with the girl who would later become my wife. It was in the nature of this love that it contained all the possibilities in the world, and that at the age of eighteen you believe you'll realize them all.

The second time I exchanged longing looks with a woman who was working at our company, a Russian engineer, and I grasped the pain of all the impossibilities that come between two married people, the cruelty of paths that have already been blocked, and the way life is sometimes a one-way street.

I was thirty-eight when I fell in love with Eytan. And in the desperation of my love, the impossible became entangled with the possible. One day I would accuse myself of crimes I would have been right to punish with death. The next day I would turn it all on its head and say, it's possible to start over. I'm in the prime of my life. I've done everything I can for my country and my family. Now I'll do something for me because until now I never knew myself.

I summoned the strength I would need to take a bold step, which had become unavoidable. I felt it in my bones as I moved like a river toward the falls, frightened and hurting and smitten.

On the threshold of the decision, Eytan showed up with a sheepish smile and bitter news: he had met someone else. Just like that. Not someone like me, he said, but a nice guy all the same. And it wasn't easy for him. He asked if there was anything he could do for me, and also promised to stay in touch, and then he turned around and disappeared like that first time.

For many months, I worked to pick up the pieces, struggling under layers of pain, anger, humiliation, and regret, trying to figure out where it had gone wrong.

Sometimes life takes care of itself, I said to Doron, the deputy commander, perched on a dune looking out over Egypt. It was the latest reserve duty. He was telling me about the crisis with his insurance business, and after that about his wife, his girlfriend, and his previous girlfriend. He was that kind of guy. "Lucky for us we got an easy time on reserves," he said. "The men couldn't take another Intifada now. And neither could we."

Only the wind spoke for a bit. The Turkish coffee was slowly coming to a boil; one bubble and then another rose to the surface of the old finjan. "You're the only commander who makes his own coffee," said Doron as I handed him a greenish mug. I told him that this was his last opportunity: next week I would bequeath the veteran coffee set to my son Amir, as a present for the start of his army service.

"A soldier already?" Doron said. "I remember when he was like this," and he held his hand to the height of little Amir. "You know how to live, you and Sarit," he added suddenly, out of the blue.

Micky the operations sergeant appeared with a question from the division. We conferred. Doron had one answer and I had another. When the reserves were this idle and so few things demanded our attention, we drew each problem out a little, in order to enjoy all its aspects. When the sergeant went away, we returned to our coffee with the proper seriousness. Doron said he hoped I'd stay in the unit. He had no desire to be battalion commander, he said, and it was good to have me by his side, always nearby. "Good friends aren't so easy to find."

I laughed and poured him a cup of coffee, saying, another war or two, tops. He stared into space and told me that he felt good doing reserve duty because he was away from all the women in his life. When I didn't respond, he mused, "Imagine a world without women. At home, not a day goes by that I don't cheat on all the women I have known with all the others, some in my mind and some with my body. But here I'm so far from all that, just having a good time, me and the guys."

I fiddled with the gas, turning the flame up and down. Two chattering birds conducted their conversation from opposite sides of a dry bush. Bored, my mind began to wander away from Doron, who was recalling romantic adventures that I had already heard long before. He had a way of killing a good story by introducing a host of unnecessary details.

Suddenly, he was wearing a smile as he turned fully toward me. "Tell me, did you ever try it with a guy?"

Shaken, I turned off the gas and looked at him. "Why?"

"Just because. You remember in the army when you gave me a weekend pass after I told you I had had sex for the first time?"

I looked searchingly at my deputy commander. His work uniform was too small on his body, which had expanded more than a little since those distant days. Sure I remember, I said.

"For a long time I've been wanting to tell you that it wasn't exactly like that. I had been fucking girls for a long time already, but that was the first time with a guy. What a wild man I was then. Who'd believe it?"

We were quiet, the desert and I, and Doron, smiling into the distance, swallowed the last of his coffee. A light breeze carried a lone cloud over the pale ridge across from us. I turned over my mug and shook the dregs onto the sand. I thought about Doron, and myself, and afterward about those eternal hills, the times we had conquered them already, and the times we would conquer them again, and again, and again.

Vadim

Translated by Ken Frieden

Son was in Moscow. Grisha. He have black eyes, little white hands move fast. He always playing at flowers. The first word he said was *snek*, that's snow. He said *snek* like a little bell. *Snek, snek.*

I have no time playing with Grisha. Lana also have no time, busy translating. Lots of work, little money. She have only little time for Grisha.

When Lana walk out, everything was black. I was black, life was black. Only Grisha was not black, he like playing at flowers. I take Grisha to big park, Lenin Park. Grisha was playing and playing, I was thinking and thinking. My head hurt—too much thinking. Why Lana walk out? What I do? I not understand. Another six months I was living in Moscow. Nothing to do there. Mother died. Small family, far away. No friends. I want to travel. Where? Could not go anyplace. To Israel, that is where. I was not wanting to be far from Grisha. But I could not stand to be in Moscow more. Was a mistake, big mistake.

In Israel, things not black, everything just gray. Sky gray, fields gray, I am gray too. I am not feeling anything.

I was living in Merkaz Klita, immigration center. Three months was in Ma'alot. Little city, little people. Then two months in Tel Aviv. Big city, little people. Then Jerusalem. Why Jerusalem? Don't know—maybe weather, maybe accident.

Was no work, also no friends. I do little this, little that. I hand out advertising newspapers. No big money. Government pay rent, then nothing. In Russia I was food engineer, here no work. I was specialist in meat thaw. No one is needing me here. They offer me this, that, little things. I never go out. I was not sad, just thinking about Grisha I was sad. But Lana don't let him talk with me on telephone. He not want to, she say. It confuse him, you know? It also hurt him—after you call, he cry. What to do? She is like that. And no money to travel. Long time I not talk with Grisha. Seven years maybe. He already big boy, I not recognize him now.

One year there was a woman. She was strange, like everyone in Israel little strange. Here I am little strange too. She is good woman. Not very beautiful, one eye like this, *nu?* Very easy I make her happy! I show to her pretty tree, she is happy. I buy flowers, she is happy. I talk good to her, she is happy. But I not talk. Hard to be talking all time. Lana always talk and talk. I am not talking. After one year, woman walk out and I'm alone again.

Had to find work. No money, nothing. Not even to buy tea. Enough! I don't want to be living on street.

Jewish agency was telling me, take course for security guard. I say good, I go to course. They ask: You was in army? I say yes, in Russia. In Russia army, I was engineer. Very good, we give you a rifle, they say. You go to shooting range, shoot ten bullets. No one see if bullets hit target. They say okay.

That's how I am working as security guard at university. First in outer gate, then in chemistry building. First day I was happy. The shirt for guards was white, new. It fit me like a suit I have in Russia. Good people in chemistry building. I walk out on lawn, go to cafeteria, go in library. I say hello to everyone that come in and out. Everyone have to come in my door.

But then not so good. On the lawn is always two students kissing. Like sculpture, like movie. Not nice to go there. Also not nice in cafeteria. Everyone who look on me know I'm immigrant from Russia. Manager of cafeteria is seeing I not eat much, because of no money. So I am not going to cafeteria. Morning I buy sandwich in another place, then I go in chemistry building, then I'm being security guard all day. I don't say to nobody hello. No one is talking to me. Sometime I go in library, but I don't like books in chemistry.

Until the day it happen. Arabs come. Arabs is always coming, lot of Arabs study in chemistry building. I don't say they're not good. I think Arabs is like Jews is like everyone all same. But Arabs are strong, more dangerous. They look on me like I do something wrong, but I'm just security guard.

What happen that day I don't know. Many Arabs come, five maybe, fast, come running. Him—I don't remember. He was first one. They tell us at security course, if there's danger, take out gun. A lot of them come and I was scared, I was alone. I take out gun. After that I don't remember. They say I shoot. I am not remembering I shoot someone. But if they say, could be. What happen after that I also don't remember. Just the police station. Police say he died. Who died? Arab died? I say, why was he running? Why he threatening me? Police say, he wasn't threatening you. He was just some kid. I kill Arab, they say. I don't know. Now I am waiting for trial. *Nu?* A trial is big thing.

Now I am just crying. All the time. Not for the Arab. I don't know this Arab. I am crying for Grisha. Arab was a boy, also Grisha a boy. Who is now guarding Grisha? How can Grisha have no father? I think on Grisha, I think on him playing at flowers. I look out my little window and see blue sky. When the sun shine, it is turning the wall red, turning the wall green, traveling on the wall till it go down.

How the World Is Run

Translated by Eva Weiss

In an alley in the industrial neighborhood of Romema, not far from Jerusalem's Central Bus Station, there is a gray, peeling building from which the world is run. There decisions are made about who will be born, who will die, who will win and lose the wars—in short, about everything.

I know this by chance. When I was looking for my insurance agent's new office, I got lost in the back alleys and needed to pee. I entered a narrow passageway between a mechanic's garage and a grocery store. There stood an unmarked building. On the ground floor there was nothing, just a security guard's desk but no security guard, so I walked up a flight of stairs. I didn't find a bathroom, and there was no one to ask. All the offices were empty, except for one, from which I heard snatches of conversation about a flood in Ecuador. I looked inside. There were three men who looked as shabby as the walls of the room. One said that there had already been a flood in Ecuador several years ago; a second said, So what? The third said that it was already terribly late and he had to leave immediately—he didn't care what they decided, so long as they did it fast. Later that evening on the news I heard there was a flood in Ecuador that day, and around three hundred people died. It's hard to believe that they took the decision so lightly, without thought, without conscience, without anything.

Although I was afraid they would catch me and inflict some small disaster on me, I continued wandering around the corridors. My whole life I had wanted to know how things happen and whether there was a guiding hand in the world, and now entirely by accident I had discovered the answer, and it was so disappointing—there was no serious-ness, no soul-searching debate. Everything was a mess; they were renovating one wing, and they had switched rooms, so no one could find the relevant files; the archives were closed, and so was the cafeteria, and there was a pervasive smell of mildew. I don't know whether they have a standard count for the number of floods per year, or a quota for the number of wounded. But in any event, their lack of seriousness stank to high heaven. No one knew what was going on; they all just wanted to get it over with and go home.

Then I walked up another flight, and in one of the rooms I saw a man who seemed to be about fifty and looked pleas-ant. I asked him if I could trouble him.

"Go ahead," he said, "just give me a minute to finish up with the epidemic."

"What epidemic?" I asked with concern.

"Of the animals," he responded, "what else?"

He's the one who decides which animals are wiped out. I asked if he had to do it. What a shame that so many spe-cies are wiped out—I remember that I once saw something about that on television.

He looked at me with astonishment and perhaps even anger. He asked me if I thought he would do this if he had any choice—it was his job, and he had some twenty-two species that he had to finish off before the end of the year and he had just started. Still, once he got into the swing of things, he would finish everything and even start with his quota for the coming year, because that's the kind of guy he was, with lots of responsibility, and he didn't want to finish another year with a backlog since he took everything seriously.

He chattered on for an hour about how conscientious he was. He talked like a saint, as though he and God were relatives. That reminded me about God, who is supposed to be pretty involved in these decisions. So I asked him about it; I wasn't shy.

"God, yes, God," he answered. "He doesn't work here anymore"—and he went right on to the next animal. He had an annoying habit of working nonstop, never taking a break. He wanted to finish off the zebras, but I succeeded in getting him off their backs. That's all we need, for God's sake, to get rid of the zebras. Instead he chose some kind of parrot from South America that I had never heard of, and I waited until he passed judgment on a type of cricket.

When he realized that I was watching him the whole time, it occurred to him to ask what I was doing there. Perhaps I was joining their department, since they were very short-staffed and had put in a request for reinforcements long ago. Possibly, I said, it's not yet clear; I want to form some impressions first. He invited me to sit down and offered me a cup of coffee, because anyway he wanted to make some. I agreed because there were several more questions that were definitely bothering me.

We started a nice chat. He told me that he had been working there since he finished his military service. The benefits were decent, but the secrecy was a bit hard to take; he himself didn't know who his employer was; they received their salary in cash, without a pay stub or any record; but what really bothered him was that they never left the office. There were no field trips and everything was extremely isolated and, ultimately, boring; there weren't any women because this was no job for a woman; and they were stuck in this corner of Jerusalem. (Of course, Jerusalem; where else would they make all of the great decisions about the world? But, wouldn't you know, he really wanted to work in Tel Aviv.) Finally, he confided that he had a dream. He very much wanted to be transferred to the Department of Ideas, to plant all the crazy thoughts in people's heads. He was dying to do it, especially with writers, and he would be thrilled if he were allowed to concoct the plots of their stories. But there were already two very senior people on the job and they wouldn't let in any new blood. On this topic we had a good conversation since we both like to read, and I've always wanted to know where writers' wild ideas come from. So there you have it.

The Life and Death of Frank 22

Translated by Marianna Barr

F rank 22" was born after I killed "Mike 25" who replaced
"Yoav 27" who succeeded "Liav 30." But unlike his
predecessors, a bunch of empty nicknames I invented for
the sake of chatting on the Internet—which were in fact
improved younger versions of myself—Frank 22 had a life of
his own, family, friends, supporting characters, super-ego,
certificates, recommendations, regrets, secret desires and
whatnot, and had I not ultimately destroyed him, he would
have taken over my life totally and God knows what else.

I invented him one night when I was feeling so down
I was willing to do anything for a one-night stand, not to
embellish reality but to ravish it. Frank was the name of a
guy I met in the army. We shared the same tent during basic
training and he occupied my wet dreams for quite a while.
In recent years I had forgotten all about him, but go figure,
you never know when an old army buddy is going to pop up
again. It all happened in a flash: Frank 22.

I made him twenty-two, my favorite age, still untarnished, still room for a few ideals.

Not before two in the morning, having cruised for quite a while as Frank 22, did it occur to me that the guy from the Tel Aviv penthouse with whom I had been chatting for an hour would eventually want to meet me. Then he would see me for the forty-two-year-old that I was and tell me to get the hell out of his face, which made me angrier than you could ever imagine. From the general characteristics I initially used to describe myself (officer-on-reserve duty, cinema lover, bisexual), Frank's character began to shape up. He was still staying with his folks but did not get along with his father at all, so he was thinking about moving in with his sister in Bat-Yam until he could start working and get a place of his own, most likely in hip Florentin. He had served in the army in an elite unit. The action in the occupied territories drove him around the bend, so during the three final months he'd served as an NCO for new recruits. He'd been writing poetry he hadn't shown anyone yet. He was a top but fantasized about being a bottom.

During the following nights, Frank broke quite a few hearts, which I don't take lightly at all. For I caused a great deal of disappointment. But had I come forth as me, I would not have generated the least bit of excitement. Young guys would not have even bothered to reply. But they sure replied to Frank 22. They chased him through all the chat rooms. They entered to inquire whether anyone had heard from him that day. His tall figure, with wide green eyes, coal-black hair, and dark skin, was reflected in the windows of their solitude, after midnight.

But what made him most human was his ex-lover, a cute American student named Brian whom he mentioned nostalgically. Brian returned to Ohio shortly after the start of the Palestinian uprising and since then had become a semi-virtual character. Frank even put on an act in which he admitted to crying occasionally, and I swear that it won him a few extra admirers.

At night fingers are light on the keyboard, words are meaningless, promises are not meant to be kept, we really aim low. But not Frank 22; he was different, more sensitive, preoccupied by existential questions, muddles, admitted to having weaknesses, took an interest in his fellow man: a palpable persuasive piece of work, far better than the novel I was busy writing back then. I was writing it during the day, but no sooner would night fall than I skipped two-three mouseclicks directly to the chats, where in digital space I would plunge like a scuba diver into the deep ocean, free from the usual pressures, amid a multitude of guys fantasizing about a certain Frank 22 who would come to their rescue.

I have to admit: Frank's appealing character, which grew and improved with each night, was far better than any of the characters I was writing about during the day, although it did not receive any literary notice or recognition of the usual kind. It opened up like a colorful parachute in the minds of horny guys like me (mostly younger, though) who were sitting at their computers during unreasonable hours in all sorts of remote places, letting my hero take control, expecting to meet him eventually: 6 feet of sensuality, 162 pounds of sweet compassionate innocence, the dream come true of night's intense hidden desires that only Frank 22 could satisfy.

I'm ashamed for not even once having the nerve to admit that I deceived them. I would always invent some lame pretext to end the conversation. Never gave my phone number but took theirs and promised to call back. They've been waiting up, after all this time, in the hope that Frank 22 might remember them. They're imagining that perhaps this very minute he's finally fixing up his new place in Florentin, placing his biology texts on the shelves, preparing for the upcoming academic year, accidentally discovering a wrinkled piece of paper on which he had scribbled their phone numbers.

I'm not sure why, but his victims were way more forgiving toward him than I was. Quite a few of them tried their luck again when he reappeared on the chat after a week or two. Only once did someone call him a "creep," and then I couldn't decide which of the two responses to use, "lay off, old fart" or "sorry, didn't mean to let you down," and ended up choosing the first, contrary to what Frank 22 would have done. Maybe that was the moment when our ways began to part and I felt that at times we had a conflict of interest. While all Frank wanted was to invent perfect narratives (which is what I do during the day but not at night), I wanted to have sex here and now; while he was a good soul who had barely begun to look inquisitively though apprehensively at his life, which was just beginning, I was one who's been there done that and could no longer be surprised by anything.

I let him have a few more gasps. I remember one night in particular. At noon I met with my new editor, who was young, energetic, dressed in a casual suit and who excited me in more ways than just the literary. After that I felt like a huge failure, which is what I tend to feel after coming in contact with people who are or seem to be accomplished.

I felt that nothing I could write would even come close to what I wanted and so, having given up on a day that would no longer amount to anything, I sat down to surf, "just for a while," which became quite a while and an incredible waste of time in which there was a desperate need to meet someone; but who, where, how? So Frank 22 proceeded with his usual ease to do what he did best—concocting heartbreaking stories. He was particularly inspired by a certain Donny from Jerusalem, of all places. "Are there gays in Jerusalem?" Frank asked, to which Donny replied "obviously"—one word, the way it's done on the Internet, which is more or less the scope and depth that people offer of themselves, but then Donny offered a whole two-line monologue: he'd just returned from a show, he sings in a choir and was feeling blue. Frank 22 thought to himself, when was the last time that anyone had admitted here to feeling blue? And now they were sharing the blues, for Frank's mother had been diagnosed with some illness, not yet clear with what, and his father who wasn't exactly famous for his sensitivity was guilt-tripping her for neglecting her household responsibilities, and Brian had not been in touch for a couple of weeks, maybe he's got someone else, and Donny kept saying, "I wish I could come and comfort you," and they were hitting it off, that's for sure, so I said to myself, you son-of-a-bitch, what have you got against this Donny, this sweet kid. And even though something in me whispered that Donny from Jerusalem, for all I knew, could just as well be a fabrication, I chose to believe his story and kept kicking myself, what has he done to you, he's just falling for a character you've made up, who could blame him? You would too in his place, and then it dawned on me that I already had developed a strange attraction toward this character I'd invented, who was totally different from me and so much nicer, and had acted out quite a few of my fantasies, and won me over with his spontaneity and his forthrightness. Only in one way did he take after me, and that was his talent for concocting plots effortlessly, as if he were pulling a thread from a spool leading into a magic forest. But I was beginning to have enough of myself, me and my fabulous act, me and my unfounded, never-ending, purposelessly spinning story.

At daybreak I went into the garden as I often do to reclaim a voice of my own or have one reclaim me, and made a few big decisions, the first of which was to kill Frank 22 and take a break from the computer. When I returned, my study already bright with daylight, I found some twenty messages from Donny, most of which consisted of the words "Frank" and "where are you." We were just the two of us in the room, which was bare and bleak, when in cold blood I wrote the ending, "Frank's dead," and turned off the computer, and could think of nothing, and only now, after a year, have I brought myself to write about him—Frank, the tall sensitive guy who, had he still been with us, would have been twenty-three today, or maybe twenty-one, anything's possible.

On the Porch

Translated by Marianna Barr

The first time Nadav Lieberman met God, he thought He was just another old *nudnik* with lots of money. It didn't bother him; quite the contrary. The type fit perfectly the profile of his favorite clientele. This happened two months after he'd gotten the brilliant idea that was going to make him rich. An idea so good it was a wonder nobody had thought of it before: start a business for teaching computers to elderly people who are afraid of new technology and are sure it's not for them.

The business caught on slowly—a customer here, a customer there. There was no shortage of old people who needed help to correspond with their distant children by e-mail or those who needed to prove that they hadn't fallen completely behind in the world's frenetic race, but only a few were willing to pay for it. Nadav was thinking of going back to work at the Holy Land Hotel front desk until business picked up—when God called him. At first he didn't say who He was. Nor did He say in the next two lessons, which were held, like the others, in the customer's home. What Nadav saw was a big house with a large courtyard with a few chickens and goats, no luxury at all. The man was an old spiritual hippie, moving about in tiny steps as if he were hanging from an invisible string. Something seemed odd from the outset, but only during their third meeting—when into the study walked an elderly angel who had forgotten his camouflage and addressed God by His ineffable name—was the truth revealed.

Nadav considered interrupting the lessons. He was, of course, alarmed. To be God's teacher—who would take such a risk? But there was in the old hippie something touching, tender, pleasant, benevolent. If in the past He had possessed less appealing qualities, they must have softened during the last couple of millennia. God asked politely to continue the lessons, even though both of them knew that the initial innocence had been lost. He explained that He had to learn how to work the computer, because He understood how impossible life nowadays was without it. So what if He had no knack for technology? He had to be in the know—and also, He admitted, He felt like looking for adventure and excitement on the Internet.

"I don't think I can teach you," Nadav apologized.

"But why?" God said, surprised.

"I'll tell you the truth. It's not just that I don't feel comfortable teaching God; there's also the problem of your ability."

"But I'm making progress, aren't I?"

"I'm not saying You aren't making progress, but the pace, I'm really sorry to have to tell you, is really slow."

God pleaded and pleaded and His request was heartbreaking. Nadav began to understand God's predicament: He was getting old, without the likelihood that He would die with dignity or die at all. No mercy, just suffering and grief, and constant good-byes from people He'd grown fond of and whose time had come, and also from places that used to be God's little heaven on Earth before they were turned into concrete jungles.

They had good talks on the porch of the big house, in the late summer breeze. God had fixed Himself a hammock where the wind could swing it (for He was not strong enough to swing it Himself) and He could reminisce. He brushed off the angels who approached Him with questions, telling them to decide for themselves. His patience was running thin. It's a good thing they had self-discipline and a sense of public mission, for they could have easily taken advantage of Him.

"Nothing is what it used to be," God grumbled, with His legs crossed and a hand playing with his wispy beard. "The rules of the game are changing. People are being stupid. The show is run by morons. And why not? Who wants a part in the leadership? Only those lusting after power and money. How could they be honest?"

He spoke of the world and His recurring disappointments, but as they got to know each other better, it seemed to Nadav that His main problem was being single in a couples' world. For God was, after all, despite His social skills, terribly alone. He would not divulge the intriguing details regarding where He came from, how and why. (He claimed He didn't know, but Nadav didn't buy it.) One thing was certain: He was second to none, He was standing alone and matchless by definition. Though the years had gone by and He seemed at peace with Himself, nothing could compensate for what was missing.

Maybe that was the reason, Nadav concluded, that God clung to him so. It wasn't the desire to learn about computers—not at all. He was harboring some hope that He might get a social life. The loneliness was driving Him insane.

As for the computer, He hardly made any progress. His fingers were not responsive. He hit the right key only once in three tries. He would confuse the letters ("I'm totally dyslexic," he admitted) and managed to break the mouse twice. The whole thing was completely pointless.

After a few more attempts, God gave up on the possibility that He would ever become computer literate, but in the meantime they grew truly close to one another, so much so that God admitted that what He really wanted to learn was how to get into the chat rooms.

"I thought I might meet people this way. I heard that virtual participants can be anything they want to be, because no one knows who you really are." Nadav liked this; he had met quite a few people in chat rooms who thought they were God, but he hadn't as yet met a god that pretended to be a human being.

A long time has passed. Nadav has replaced his computer twice and his girlfriend three times. Things with God have settled into an easygoing routine: They meet at least once or twice a week. The thing they most enjoy doing together is watching films. Each time they watch a sad movie, God gets sentimental and Nadav has to swear that he won't abandon Him. God is stuck with His Godliness and Nadav continues to ponder the dilemmas of blind dates and ever-changing jobs.

"Your life is like a soap opera," God laughs, and Nadav thanks God for the small favors in what is otherwise such a sad world.

Utterly Nameless

Translated by Michael Swirsky

I put the tray down on the table, take off my backpack, and look up at the big window of the cafeteria, through which I can see the courtyard between Humanities and Social Sciences and the lawn outside Education. It's the only open vista I have seen for years now. Someone goes by with a cup in her hand, headed for the corner table. At first I pay no attention, but seeing her float ever so lightly past that outdoor scene reminds me of something. I look at her face and—no, it can't be—God, it's Millie, my ex-girlfriend, the one I've been dreaming about all these years. Millie herself, in a tailored maroon suit and an avocado-green velour scarf, her blonde hair carefully coiffed. I would pretend not to see her, but I can't. We're practically the only ones on this side of the cafeteria, and she's already looking up, perhaps sensing that someone is looking her way, and then, of course, she sees me.

Actually, I don't know what she sees. Certainly not the Yohai she remembers. And not the person I should have become by now. What she sees is an embarrassing combination of pants that are too long and a beige shirt that's none too clean, a nerdy pair of glasses I've been using this last month since my regular ones broke, an unkempt beard, and the face of someone who doesn't know what he wants from himself. I've been waiting all these years for this moment, and when it comes I'm not even decently dressed.

My heart is pounding wildly, but she—it's hard to make out under her makeup what exactly she's feeling. Only a slight, fishlike frown betrays some tension. It was always hard to tell what was going on inside her head because she didn't talk much. Once, just once, she talked too much. It was during our last conversation, ten years ago, when she threw the whole truth in my face, uncensored. And ever since, I've known more than I should.

What I always thought would happen when we met again was that I would answer everything she'd said to me back then. The answer has been jelling in my mind all these years, measured and fair, but probably this isn't my day.

"Yohai?!"

"Millie! What a surprise!"

"You look good," she says, lying. Now it's my turn to say something about the way she looks, at least a small compliment about the scarf, but I can't bring myself to do it. I'm flustered by her successful, well-groomed appearance. You can tell right away she's in a good place, and this is a bad way to begin this encounter, which, according to all the scripts, was supposed to be the other way around, with her down and out and me at my peak. Next will come the story about where we've been and what we've been doing. That's what it will be, after all, a story, or rather two stories, each five minutes long, or hers five and mine ten, since I'm the wordy type and she isn't, even though her degree was in linguistics. A story is only a story, and like all stories it will be made up of things that really happened and some that may not have.

She can present herself as being even more successful than she really is, or she can put in a lot of scenic description and skimp on the important details, or she might work me into her story: "And then I thought of getting in touch with you" or "It reminded me of you" or "Too bad you weren't there."

"What are you doing here?"

"What am I doing here?!" I say. "What are *you* doing here?! Aren't you studying in America?"

"I recently finished my doctorate. We just got back to Israel two weeks ago."

"Who's 'we'?"

"You knew I got married."

"No. To whom?"

To whom—that's what comes out. To whom.

I never thought that she'd do it. That she'd do it to me. That she'd get married, but not to me. Not that I thought she wouldn't get married, not in the sense of "she won't get married," but more in the sense of . . . I didn't think so. It didn't seem like a possibility to me.

I fantasized that we'd get back together. Every foray I ever made, every date with a woman, was with her in mind. How I would explain it to her, or what she would say if she knew. Only now that I have actually met up with her do I understand how detached I was from reality. Almost ten years have gone by, and she's gotten herself a life. She's married. Of the two of us, it is I who am stumbling in the dark.

She was what my mother called a "perpetual student." Mother was always against her, even before we went to university. And the fact that I homed in on her despite Mother's advice may also have been a way of rebelling against Mother and her fixed views. But in the meantime, Mother's gone, and there's no one left to rebel against. Not even the small pleasure—the only pleasure I can imagine in this situation—of calling her and telling her that Millie has received a doctorate. If Mother could hear that, she would just say Millie had bought her degree. And if I also told her Millie had gotten married, she would say her husband had bought it for her. Mother would fabricate a whole story. And what a story. She was a great storyteller, Mother was. And what she especially loved was to invent sad endings to her stories. Mother hated happy endings. She enjoyed the difficult kind, full of suffering and pain. Unfortunately, that's how her own story ended.

But Millie has won. She's got what I lost: determination, optimism. It's true you can see a hint of wrinkling around her mouth, but all in all she's one of those women who get more beautiful as they age. She looks settled, strong, mature. All the things we were once sure she would never be. Or was it only I who thought so? Maybe she knew even then that she would go far. Maybe she decided, after we separated, to put her energies into making something of herself rather than pouring them into a guy with delusions of grandeur who would simply weigh her down.

"What are you up to?" she asks with interest.

"Today?"

"In general."

"You want the truth?"

"Yes, the truth. We want to be truthful, don't we?"

That's not fair. She wasn't someone who always told the truth. She would lapse into silences as long as the coastline, followed by airy, noncommittal statements that left you in the dark as to what she was actually thinking. I was the one who said we should tell each other everything. We argued about this quite a bit. I was committed to trust and honesty in our relationship, or something exalted like that. I no longer remember exactly what ideal it was that I adopted or invented, only that I believed in it religiously. But she—she wanted a home, children, a family, not heart-to-heart talks at three in the morning. Okay, she could put up with the fact that she had a kind of live-in intellectual. She was always willing to listen to my ruminations, to look as though she were thinking them over, even to say yes now and then. And now she's suggesting nonchalantly that I tell the truth, and she sounds so natural saying it. I have to get used to the fact that she speaks differently now, that everything is different.

"You remember I was thinking of going on to an M.A. in math," I say. "Well, I ended up doing one in philosophy, and also in psychology. You must have heard."

"No."

"You haven't stayed in touch with anyone?"

"Here and there. Not for a long time."

"But you must have asked what happened to me."

She looks at me for a moment, weighing her response. Once I was the stage on which her life was being played out. Now she owes me nothing. But I assume she doesn't want to hurt me, either.

"Maybe I preferred not to ask. I'm not sure."

I take a breath.

"I didn't know you were planning to do a doctorate," I say. "In what field?"

"Linguistics."

"What did you write about, exactly?"

"The existential 'there,'" she says.

I can't help laughing, and she smiles a little. How could she not? The existential "there." Isn't that something! I remember her bringing home a hefty tome once, bigger than a telephone book, on the subject of the existential "there." I asked her what it meant, and she explained that it was the "there" of "There's a boy in the garden." Or, "There's a man who loves his wife." Which is very different from the "there" of "He isn't there." Or of "I would have liked him to be there."

These are the very examples she used. I remember them to this day. I couldn't believe someone had written a whole book about such nonsense. Are we making such fools of ourselves in the august corridors of the university? Don't we have anything more important to do? That's more or less what I told her at the time.

And now she's written a dissertation about it, and it's probably even thicker than the book she'd brought with her then. I remember it very well. It had a bluish-green binding, and its thickness offered one big advantage: I could use it to prop up the bed to avoid heartburn. We had to pay a library fine, but it was worth it. So maybe the whole point of her dissertation was to defy me? No. I'm evidently going to have to get over the idea that she's living her life in relation to me. It seems that she's living her life in relation to her life, and for her that's real progress.

"So you're back in Jerusalem?" I ask.

"Yes."

"Have you found a job?"

"They've given me two courses to teach in the department. They still haven't promised, but there's a chance of a real position next year."

That's really too much. A position at the university! The first one in years, and it's Millie Shashua who's getting it! What stands between me and a position there is the doctorate I haven't done, the analysis I haven't started, and who knows what else. And for her they're creating a position! Look at her, and look at me.

I debate whether to ask her what her husband does. I'm not sure I can take another success story.

"What does your husband do?"

The word *husband* sticks in my throat, no two ways about it.

"He's a doctor. He hasn't found work here yet, but he's not in a hurry. He wants to take a break."

I'd like to know what he has to take a break from, but it's better not to ask. The very fact that there's a husband in the picture is enough. And a doctor, to boot.

"And you? You haven't told me anything. Are you still studying?"

"There's not much to tell. I haven't gone on for my doctorate, for the time being, anyway. I worked for some years at the National Library, and then I resigned."

"Why did you resign?"

"I had too many disagreements with them about how to run things. It made me angry to see how casually they treated our cultural treasures."

Cultural treasures. That's what I said. If it came across as stuffy, well, that's me. From what sleeve did I suddenly pull out cultural treasures? What had actually happened was a quarrel with two people, one of them the boss, and I couldn't just swallow my idiotic pride and get on with it. Get on with it? I could hardly breathe. For two weeks, I stayed home and waited for someone to call and ask me to come back to work. But no one ever called.

"And what are you doing now?"

I don't know how to answer. The truth is that I'm not doing anything now. For months, I've gone around with plans to focus again on writing poetry, on reconnecting with the muse that might be singing within me. (It isn't just an invention of mine that I'm a poet, or that I look like one. I've always been told that. When you see my troubled face, with the beard, the glasses, and the deep-blue eyes, it's hard not to think of me as a poet. At one time, they thought me handsome.)

"The truth is, I'm sort of trying to find myself."

No sooner have I gotten the sentence out than I regret it and try to catch it in midair and bring it back, but it's already circulating freely throughout the cafeteria. Luckily, she says nothing. She's as tactful as ever. She understands me. That, at least.

Why did I have to tell her I was trying to find myself? It's not as if we were sitting and having a real conversation. We're not even sitting. We're still standing, she with a cup in her hand and I leaning on a chair that has no idea why I've latched onto it. But this chair is playing a major role in our drama. Without it, I would already have fallen to the floor. Trying to find myself. What will she think now?

"Here, let me give you our phone number. We're renting a place in Old Katamon. Why don't you come and visit? I'm sure Werner would be happy to meet you."

Werner. Disgusting name.

There's something I haven't asked yet, and I'm wondering if I should. About children.

"Do you have any kids?"

"Two. Shai is already six and a half, and Naama is four."

She gives me a slightly anxious look. The children—that's what brings this conversation to the breaking point. Now she gulps down the whole cup of coffee and tells me to get in touch. The odd thing is, she seems to mean it.

So what does it do to me, this new look of hers? I think about it all the way home on the endless number 9 bus line, and afterward, sitting on the porch with my feet propped up on the railing and my head leaning against the wall. Is she attractive or not? That's the question. Her face has filled out, and the rest of her body, too, has acquired padding and upholstery. It's not the girlish figure it once was. But on the other hand, she is more of a woman this way. Could I be aroused by this new look of hers? And who am I going to think about now in my fantasies, the girl she was or the blonde woman in the cafeteria? Will I mix the two images together? Will the new Millie cancel out the old one in my mind? They can't possibly complement one another. They can only exist apart. One or the other.

The boys used to get excited when they saw her dance. She was the one everyone at the party looked at. It was she who set the pace, not the old-fashioned phonographs we had then. Oh, how much we've been through since then. Who cares about such things anymore? And the raspy loud-speaker in the yard where the scout troop met. Tuesday evenings we used to go to folk dancing. That's where I fell in love with her. I didn't know how to dance, but I went with the guys week after week to see the girls dance. I had my eye on her right from the start. I'd spend hours looking at her, and then at night I would masturbate to my memories, plotting to murder the redhead who had been dancing with her. Finally, I asked my older sister to teach me how to dance. Two good things came out of this. One, my sister and I became friends. (Okay, maybe it wasn't friendship, more like a covenant, a pact, a partnership.) And two, after a month I was able to dance with Millie. It was during *Shuv ha'eder noher* that she looked at me for the first time. She had no choice: there was a step where she had to look to the right. And little by little she got used to me. It was a month later, during *Shir sameah*, that I began to feel electricity in the grip of her hand.

She always thought she had fallen in love with me first, and she never believed me when I told her it had all been planned. Surely she would never have just fallen for me. Why would a girl who danced like her even look at me?

How I loved to dance with her! How supple she was. Sometimes she would leap into midair, leap and never come down. And me, my insides would jump. But afterward, when we went for a walk in the neighborhood, she became a different person: reticent, reflective. I thought it was beautiful. And I had enough to say for the both of us.

I started plotting how to get her into bed, to seduce her one way or another. I had in mind to invite her to my aunt and uncle's house up north. They had been so kind as to give a room with a double bed to my sister and her boyfriend the soldier, and it had worked well for her. Too well. What resulted was an abortion. But Millie surprised me. I didn't have to persuade her at all. With her parents in the house, she put me in her own bed, locked the door, and with confident movements, taught us both how it was done. She has an inborn gift for all things of the body. I was in such a state of shock that it was only the following day that I realized how momentous the occasion had been.

She was like two different people. She could be a tiger at times. But when she was serious, which was most of the time, she was kind of gloomy. Or, as I told her when we quarreled, a bit dead. I didn't think it was such a big insult. My friends said things to their girlfriends that were a million times worse. But evidently she was terribly offended, or at least that was the conclusion I came to when she assaulted me with her parting speech in the house on Shim'oni Street, with her parents waiting downstairs in the car. She told me it was I who was dead. Dead as a human being, and dead to her.

I had hoped for another round with Millie's wonderful body. But it was no longer mine. Yet her fantastic suppleness stayed in my mind, projected, when needed, like a well-chosen film. I could visualize her at will in a thousand different poses.

But now there's nothing left of this suppleness. She's practically fat. Why practically? She *is* fat. In bed, she's probably nothing special. She looks like someone you have to fuss over. She is the center of attention, she is the object. She probably doesn't move much. Or at least so it pleases me to think. I like to think Mr. Werner will never get what I did.

After we separated, I was devastated. I lost my appetite. I languished for hours in front of the TV without caring what I watched. But I didn't do too badly with girls. For a year or two, I managed to tumble into quite a few beds. Except that it got more and more boring. It turned out that sex could be awfully dull without Millie. One of my regulars caught on to the fact that we weren't alone in bed. She asked questions all the time: "What are you thinking about?" "What are you feeling?" and so on. Once she got on my nerves so much that, against my best interests, I told her the truth. No, I don't really love you. Yes, you remind me of someone else. Yes, of my former girlfriend. What's her name? Her name is Millie. Yes, she's pretty. Yes, you're pretty too. No, she's prettier. But you do remind me a bit of her. Yes, I think about her when I'm with you.

"You can't come without thinking of her, can you?"

"That's right," I answered.

"Pervert."

And with that she threw me out, without even letting me come.

The discovery that I couldn't come without Millie surprised me. It's the kind of thing you know but don't really know, until you're hit over the head with it.

It ran counter to my theories. I always believed that the way we men were made, we weren't programmed to be with just one woman. It just didn't work that way. A man, I thought, is by nature a hunter, and it's all a matter of chance: Millie or Tillie or Lily, whoever you latch onto, whoever builds her nest around you, whoever it works out with. But one, two, three years went by, and Millie still hadn't flown away from the nest in my head. Now it's been ten years. What have I been doing with myself all these years? I've written a poem.

Exactly one poem.

I started writing it while I was still with Millie. I never showed it to her. I didn't want her to see it until it was done. But it was never good enough. And there were always distractions. Between my poem and life's demands, the poor poem always lost out. Once, after we had had a fight, I rewrote it, and it was just then that I was nearly satisfied with it. I put it aside and then came back to it the first Shabbat I spent alone, after she was gone. I took my notebook, went out to the Valley of the Cross, settled against a tree, and for half a day held my pen over the first line. My feeling then was that the poem had to say everything, all the big things I was feeling, or even more than that, to tell me what I was feeling, to express the distress and the helplessness as well as the beauty of the special moments Millie and I had had together.

For a year it lay in my drawer. Then I bought a computer. When I went to copy it into the computer, it didn't seem worth the effort. So I copied just the title and the opening line. After a while, I deleted the title. It seemed better without one. But I had a lot of second thoughts about whether it would be better without the title, just with some asterisks, the way it sometimes is in books. It wasn't a simple decision. I anguished over it for weeks.

In the end, I decided not to give it a title of any kind, and after a while I deleted the first line too. What was left was a blank document. But it was still the same poem, because I knew more or less where it was supposed to go; I just didn't know how to get there. Over the years it continued to crystallize. It went through all kinds of phases. At one point it was short, another time long. First it was amusing, then depressing. Over the last year I've spent quite a bit of time working on it, but I'm still not happy with it. It's hard for me to make the necessary compromises. Like the compromises in life. This constant tension between what is desired, what is important, what is possible, and what *is*. It's a tension I'm not built for.

I haven't got the strength to make dinner. Not even cornflakes. I go inside, get an apple, and head back to the porch. In a little while it'll be dark. At the yeshiva next door, they're reciting the afternoon service. I love to hear them praying. I love them altogether. That is, I hate them too—they don't serve in the army and all that—but I love them all the same. I see them as heroes in a way. It's nothing short of heroic to stay in the fifteenth century when the twenty-first is moving ahead full steam. Not to go to movies. Not to make passes at girls. How, how do they do it? All they have to do is wag a little finger, raise an eyebrow, or sniff the air, and a girl will look their way! But it's as if they neither see nor hear a thing. They turn up the volume of their prayers and force everyone around to listen to them. Sometimes I feel like trying to talk to one of them. But what would I say?

It's evening now. I'm still in the same position, my feet on the porch railing. I'm hungry. I'm terribly sad. The sight of Millie today lingers all around me, and she's not the person I once knew, nothing like what she was for me all those years. And there's no chance that we'll run into one another again and that, out of the blue, she'll come home with me to make love.

There's a breeze, and it's dark out. In the yeshiva, everyone's gone, but a light is still burning. They never turn off the lights, maybe because the government pays their electric bills too. It's not because they're afraid of burglars. What's to steal there? God?

I have no idea what to do with myself. It's chilly out, but I don't feel like going in. I'm not up to reading. I'm certainly not interested in watching talking heads on TV. There's no one I feel comfortable getting in touch with to tell what happened to me today. The real problem is, I can't even get in touch with myself. There's nothing but darkness, darkness in every direction. I'm starting to get a headache, I'm hungry, I'm cold, my thoughts are getting tangled up, and of all the many and varied things I've learned in my life—great heaps of knowledge acquired at huge effort, wonderful passages of literature that I've fallen in love with, wisdom garnered from thinkers of all ages—there's nothing that can help me, nothing that can extricate me from this pit.

I keep coming back to the conversation I had with myself after that speech of Millie's. How can you tell what another person is thinking? We lived together for two and a half years, and we had innumerable talks. I thought I knew everything there was to know about her. I thought she loved me. Then, at the end, she threw in my face that she had never loved me and didn't think I loved her. That everything we had together had, in fact, been a lie, a lie that suited both of us. That's what she said, after everything we had together.

But today, today she tells me it's important to be truthful.

So how can you tell what another person is thinking? What lies behind the loving gaze? What is true in this world? How do you know?

I tried in my poem to grapple with these questions, but nothing came of it. I asked myself why my words hadn't helped even me. Could she have been right? Could it all be a lie? Could I have fooled myself, too? Could I still be fooling myself? Could I be fooling myself even now, as I think these thoughts? Am I being a friend to myself or a traitor? How is one to know?

Words cannot be trusted. I've stopped reading poetry.

Several days go by this way. I go from my bed to the porch and back, my hours are irregular, I eat only cornflakes. I scratch myself and don't bathe. My encounter with Millie keeps coming back to me. Everything I said and she said and I replied. My head is full of better lines than the ones I used. The things I really should have told her. Things that could have upset her annoying equanimity. What I am to her: merely a youthful mistake. An episode. I try to guess what role I play in the story of her life. Let's say she's telling someone her story. I might get one sentence, something like, "I had a serious boyfriend, but I broke up with him when I realized nothing would ever come of it." Or maybe I wouldn't even get that.

I've got no energy. No ideas. Nobody. Nothing. An absolute desert. I've shut myself in and can't escape. Not that I'm not looking for a way out. I know I've got to find the strength to pull myself up by my hair. But I haven't done it. At night I fall asleep, wake up, fall asleep again.

I have a terrible dream. In the dream, I ask permission to end my life, but the judge, who is me, won't allow it. So I go to see my father. Who is also me. And he completely ignores me. It's as if I weren't there. So I walk and walk and walk until I get to an open area, where I lie down on the sand and fall asleep. I dream I'm a cook. I'm making a wonderful meal, with all the spices in the world. My children are coming to eat. There are at least a hundred of them, but not one of them likes the meal I've prepared. Finally, it gets dark and I'm left completely alone and forlorn, utterly forlorn.

Come Friday, I begin to worry: maybe the worst is yet to come, maybe it will come on Shabbat. Shabbat is a bad time for people who are alone. A number of friends invite me to eat with them, but I don't answer the messages they leave on the machine. Once, I turn on the TV, see the speaker of Parliament, and turn it right off. I turn it on again and watch a little of a program about snakes. An expert is talking about them affectionately, stroking them, complaining about the way urban development is encroaching on their living space. Soon there will be a world without rattlesnakes—that's what he calls his friends, rattlesnakes—and then what?

I don't know, and I fall asleep. But not for long. I awaken and doze off, awaken and doze off. At dawn, I go back out to the porch, put my feet up on the railing, and look around.

The birds are busy with their morning chores. It's nice to hear them. Little by little, things are becoming clearer. My head aches, but something inside has calmed down. I'm not so crazy, I'm not. I just have to clean myself out. To get rid of . . . of. . . .

The sun has already risen over the yeshiva. The first boys are showing up. I hear voices. One of them comes out into the yard and walks around. He doesn't see me. They never see me. But I see him.

"Come here," I call out. He looks around, still not seeing me. I stand up.

"Hey," I shout. Now he catches sight of me.

"You're going to be Millie now."

"What?"

I look at him and take a deep breath. I know exactly what I'm going to do.

"Listen carefully. I want you to understand me. I asked you day after day what was going on, what you were feeling, whether something was missing, whether there was something I should be doing that I wasn't, or something I was doing that I shouldn't. And what did you say? Nothing. Silence. The silence of the grave."

"Do you need something?" he asks, startled. But I pay no attention to what he's saying. It's not important. Other boys are gathering around.

"You told me I should have understood without being told. But why? And what did you mean about 'freeing' you? Freeing you from what? You didn't tell me anything! It was only on that last day that you talked to me. That speech of yours, how it hurt. Like a bullet to the heart. You said I was all wrapped up in myself and didn't even see you. Yes, I am, but with you I was a different person!"

"Why don't you go inside?" he says. "You should take a drink of water."

But what he says just provokes me to go on.

"How dare you answer me! You threw me out without giving me a chance, that's what you did. You did your practicing on me, and then you started your life. It turns out it was you who were all wrapped up in yourself. You quietly made yourself into a victim, without sharing with me any of what was happening to you."

I go out of the porch into the yard, approach the fence, and kneel down. The boy's face looks troubled. His friends are talking to him, but he pushes them away, listening to me.

"You know what? I love you. That's what you don't get. I always did, and I always will, no matter what happens." I can't hold back my tears. If Millie were there she'd be impressed. She's never seen me cry.

"You, Millie, you. It's you I love. And one more thing."

"Yes," he says, "tell me."

"You loved me too. Even if you had to say, at the end, that you didn't—you did. I don't know how I know, but I do. Period."

It's slowly getting quieter. His friends are moving off, leaving him by himself, some ten yards away, a boy in black pants and a white shirt. If there were no fence between us we might get closer. After a few minutes, he begins to speak.

"Go take a rest now. If you need something, call me. Call 'Millie,' and I'll come out. Okay?"

I look at him for a moment, trying to register his features so that I can pick him out from the crowd of yeshiva students. I want to thank him for this moment, but I've lost my voice. I just nod.

"Everything will be all right now," he says, and then, after a moment's reflection, he adds, "God willing."

Before disappearing he turns and waves, and I wave back.

The National Library

Translated by Ken Frieden

Barry and Liz are close friends of close friends. As soon as I received the first e-mail regarding them, it was obvious that, along with the pleasure of meeting such nice and interesting people, there would also be challenges. I would have to find a hotel room for them, arrange an itinerary of trips and meetings, and also feed them occasionally. All of this would not exonerate me from the primal sin: that I hadn't offered to put them up in my home—although everyone knows that I have an extra bedroom that is equipped for visits just like this.

When they arrived I discovered that Barry and Liz are indeed wonderful people who carried with them a breath of fresh air from the wide world. I paid in full for our first meal and suggested that we meet again in two days. As the first guided tour, I chose the university campus at Givat Ram, which I like so much. I patiently explained to them where they should catch bus 4A and exactly where we would meet. (I have also been a tourist and I know how unpleasant it is to search for a nonexistent address after you've been told again and again how easy it is to find.)

They looked like people who would arrive on time, so when they were late it occurred to me to check whether bus 4A really does go to Givat Ram. In the years since I studied there, perhaps changes had taken place in the Egged bus lines, or in the circuitous pathways of my brain. As usual, the latter and worse possibility turned out to be true. 4A is an excellent bus, but it never dreamed of going to Givat Ram.

Shaken by my sloppiness and by its probable consequences, I waited at our designated meeting point, expecting the worst. I guessed what was going to happen: Barry and Liz would arrive in a taxi with frayed nerves, after a long trip going the wrong way. They'd try to accept my sincere apology, but in their condition they wouldn't be able to enjoy the tour or anything else. Instead of getting to know the charming people I had been promised, I would meet their exhausted, dark shadows. Blockhead that I am, couldn't I check before I showed off my expertise?

My script was correct, in general, except that Barry emerged from the taxi alone. He did look broken, a faded image of the tall and smiling person I had met two days earlier. Even before he opened his mouth, it was clear that the more sensitive Liz had not withstood the hardships of the journey and had left for the hotel I had labored to find for them. No doubt she had cursed me, her husband, and all of the Jewish people (which she had joined only recently, and now had yet another good reason to regret it).

This occurrence would not have been so bad, except that the day before they'd had a similar mishap, which lasted several hours. The locals confused them with faulty explanations, sent them on the wrong buses going in the wrong direction. This disconcerting process revealed the true face of the Israeli: a compulsive and unstoppable chatterbox. Oy, I thought, am I also like that?

As we walked along the paths of the campus trying to forget the trauma, old acquaintances sprouted up in front of us—the writer and storyteller Yosl Birstein and his wife Marganit. It occurred to me that meeting the important author would to some extent patch things over with Barry, who is a professor of literature. I introduced them and congratulated Yosl on his new book, which had received an excellent review in the weekend newspaper.

In honor of the guest, Yosl burst into conversation in English and immediately shared with us some of his experiences as a writer.

"What I like is to write about people I meet on the bus."

Before my eyes, the small miracle I imagined started to unravel.

"There's nothing more pleasant than spending time on a bus," he continued with unstoppable momentum, while his bald head shone in the winter sun and the tragicomic lines of his face lit up. "You travel comfortably, meet people, hear stories beyond your wildest dreams, and when it's over not only did you enjoy the trip, but you have filled your stomach with excellent new plots."

"Certainly," Barry said with a blank expression as I cursed my bad luck.

"The bus," Yosl said with delight, and waved his hands like the conductor of an orchestra, "is the whole world. At a traffic light, between red and green, I can hear an entire life story, and sometimes even two!"

"Beautiful."

"And even if I forget to get off at the right stop," Yosl exulted, his voice ringing with a Yiddish inflection, "or if

I take the wrong bus, I get off twice as satisfied. The first time going, the second time returning! No story is more successful than one that comes to you willy-nilly." Here his gleaming face froze, as if he were a pantomime artist who has reached his climax and is waiting for the applause.

"Sure," Barry assented, polite to the very end, and I dragged him away from there in order not to grate any more on his worn nerves.

I thought about Yosl, the great artist, and his sense of timing. His stories, like the characters that populate them, are interwoven in perfect harmony, turning and winding like cogs in a magnificent apparatus. How did he know to wander out on a side path of Givat Ram, ready and waiting to play his unique role in my story?

Meanwhile, it had become cooler outside. I showed Barry the National Library, wrapped in a blanket of dark vines. He went to phone Liz, and as I sat there overlooking the landscape I love, among the refreshing scents I remember from childhood, the opening lines of this story took shape in my head.

Alone

Translated by Terri Klein
and Sarah Rubinfeld

Our Subaru pulled out in the direction of the traffic signal with blinking emergency lights. This is Yuval's way of signaling to me "See you later" when I look out from the balcony. It's cute, even after all these years.

He suggested that I join him for a conference on management methods at Hotel Moriah in Sodom, but I was already exhausted from the ostentation at public events in his line of work. We were like a walking flag: a couple of men who stuck out in everyone's eyes, confirming some people's liberal image of themselves, testing others, and driving the rest crazy. Instead of rushing around between boring workshops at the Dead Sea, I rejoiced in the opportunity to do all the things I never get around to doing, like putting the photo album in order or reading a book. And the main thing was to be alone a little bit, at last.

On the way to make myself coffee, I disconnected the telephone in order to ensure my tranquility. I made the coffee last half an hour. I listened to the new Yael Levi CD and gazed up, questioning, at the little square of sky above Tel Aviv, in which there lay a hazy promise of rain. Me, I'm crazy about winter.

With the end of the coffee, cold and bitter, the sweet satisfaction began to seep out of a Shabbat by myself. In its place troublesome doubts stole in. Why didn't I join him, after all? Surely I could have done almost all the things that I planned there, in the hotel, in a pleasant room with a wonderful view and meals on the expense account, across from my best friend.

After this thought, my disappointment in myself infiltrated: I've been waiting a long time for an opportunity to be alone, and when such an opportunity arises I am attacked by wintry weariness. What's going on?

I went over to the other armchair and weighed things slowly. Maybe I simply wasn't used to being alone. Like a child, after an hour or two, I would calm down a little and concentrate on some sort of work. I took out the green photo album that I bought toward the end of the week, and felt for the promising slipperiness of the plastic pages. The album gazed at me and I at it. Finally I put it aside, next to three books that had quarreled for a long time already—in vain—over which would be read first.

The CD started over again, and this time the songs were sadder. I reconnected the telephone; a pleasant intrusion might help after all.

I spent the remainder of the day pacing nervously, dusting here and there, trying to read, and again and again sneaking to the refrigerator and the cookie jar.

The sunset came and completed my melancholy. From the plastic chair on the balcony, the boring lives of the neighbors now looked full of flavor and activities. With the coming of night, a delicate scent of Erev Shabbat spread in the air, and with it came yearnings for something warm and distant, which had accumulated in the genetic material and begged to break out, particularly now, as if they knew that I was alone, an easy and fragile target.

Yuval called in high spirits as soon as he arrived at the Dead Sea. I said that I felt good and I was reading a lot. Why should he worry? He said that they had already started with the lectures and in the evening there would be a show, and I envied him, because he was in a hotel at the Dead Sea with colleagues from work and entertainment and shows in the evening while I was alone. I envy him a lot, especially when he's far away.

I finished yesterday's casserole in big gulps and went downstairs. The smells from all the windows had an even better aroma, homey and pleasant. The street, in the middle of Tel Aviv, bathed in the intimacy of Shabbat. On our balcony appeared only the two plastic chairs, wrapped in a great darkness.

I went out to the avenue and stared at the city lights. On other days, evening walks have a good influence on me. The city speaks with me in a blaze of lights and colors and sounds and all the other people are my partners, sharing the view and the culture and the era. But that night their presence—together—accentuated my own loneliness.

I returned home, and, as if determined to overtake myself before I had time to forbid it, I turned on the television. Added to the noises of the city was the news, thrusting itself at me, and requesting an answer: how is it that all over the world very important things are taking place, while I am pondering my own little loneliness?

In fact, I continued this conversation, putting on pajamas in our bedroom, you're really not alone. What is it, after all, this aloneness? You are also alone when you are together, and you are together also when you are alone. No one will ever force you out of your loneliness inside yourself. Human connections on any level are nothing but an illusion. Certainly there is nothing in them to dispel existential loneliness. After all, there are at least ten good people who care about me, maybe twenty, even if they are not here this minute.

The more you learn to manage with yourself alone, the more complete a person you will become. This way, as the paradox goes, you will be more appealing to others.

Still arguing with myself, I fell asleep. In the morning I woke up tired from the conflict of the night.

The friends I called were screening messages with their answering machines, and only one living voice answered me—Irit from Ramat Gan, drowsy, who promised to call back later.

I got out of my morning shower a little encouraged, wrapped in Yuval's soft, blue bathrobe. I prepared a first coffee and went over the two weekend newspapers. I won't admit to this even under torture, but I skipped over all the articles for lack of patience and read every word of the gossip column.

The neighbors on the opposite balcony were gathered for breakfast. In a red silk nightgown, the wife was walking in and out with a tray and mugs. As usual, her husband didn't help her. Two of the children, who look alike and are great laughers, seated at opposite ends of the table so that they wouldn't quarrel, were digging into their plates with fervor. I hoped the rain would drive them inside, and got mad at myself that loneliness exposed my evil side.

Seated on the carpet, I returned to the analysis of my situation from where I left off during the night. I recalled that when I was little I frequently felt lonely, and then I used to burst into tears. Also after the army there was a year like that. First, weeks would pass before I made contact with anyone; and there were those forced social gatherings that were only painful reminders of my lack of connection. More than I looked forward to them, I couldn't wait for them to end.

Since Yuval showed up on the scene, my life had changed so completely that I almost forgot who I was before.

Irit returned my call. "Are you sick?" she demanded. "You sound terrible."

"Just a little tired," I lied.

After her came telephone calls from the friends who came out from behind their answering machines.

"You sound pretty down," said one.

Another wondered, "Are you okay?"

A third inquired, "What are you doing at home? Aren't you two at the Dead Sea?" I said that I had a little cold.

In the afternoon there was a piercing knock on the door. Irit appeared with fruit salad, sat herself down and told a long funny story about her third and final failure in the psychology exam. In the middle of the story, there was another knock and with it Eran and Uri. Inside of two hours the whole gang showed up, reminding me that there are friends in the world. Until I quickly forgot why I felt what I felt, and inside the tumult someone else emerged in me, sociable and light.

Toward evening, I remained alone, appeased.

I turned to cook something. Yuval arrived in the middle and said, "You sounded miserable on the telephone, so

I decided to leave early." He sent a wondering look to the large bowl being filled on the kitchen table. "How come Chanukah latkes?" I laughed too, because according to the book I was preparing "potato pancakes."

At night I began to arrange the first pages in the photo album. From before Yuval there are only a few photos, as if I didn't want to immortalize what was then. Only when he entered my life did I become an enthusiastic photographer, trying to document every moment. Even our first night is preserved: the smile that's before, the smile that's after.

When I finished arranging the pictures from our trip to Italy, I stood up in the corner of the bedroom and looked at the sleeping Yuval as he spread out diagonally, relaxed, his cheek touching the sheet, his mouth open a little. Cute. Don't leave me alone, I pleaded in a whisper, only not alone.

Keeping Kosher

Translated by David Ehrlich

The second time that Nir and I did the weekly shopping in the supermarket together, I realized that without saying so, we had become a couple. It was then that the woman from the cheese section asked what our connection was. I don't know what she had in mind when she asked that. Nir pulled himself together first. "He's my brother." She smiled: "How nice. I would have never been able to tell. You don't look alike at all." "Well, we have different fathers, because Mom got divorced." So she threw in another piece of cheddar cheese. The following week he told her that our parents lived abroad, and another time, when we bought some fancy French cheese for our anniversary, he shared with her that our folks were coming for a visit.

I hate him when he does this.

With the woman from the meat section, he's also connected. To her he said (because she too had asked): "He's my uncle." ("Such a young uncle?")

The meat and the dairy are not so far apart at our supermarket, and I worry that someday the two women might meet up and compare what they know about us.

I'd like to live in a place where everybody knows the same thing about me, and it doesn't make any difference to them.

And in the meantime I let him do the weekly shopping on his own. He buys, I cook, he tells them stories; and in the end I also cook up the stories.

It's All Right

Translated by Ben Lerman

Once a month, according to the Hebrew calendar, Mom and Dad write me a letter from Israel. Here in Moab, Utah, I tear open the envelope with my fingers, too rushed to look for a knife, and put a small pile of news on the kitchen counter. First comes a detailed portrait of the weather in Mom's fine, precise hand. After that are the stories about the grandchildren, and then the uncles and the aunts, and in the end a little news from the yard.

The mulberry tree is sick.

I close my eyes and imagine the little courtyard in Holon, the way it looks from the round table on the porch. I see every leaf, every grasshopper and beetle. We used to have some sad, reddish flowers that could never adapt to the harsh soil, but my father, a strong man, fussed over them in his stubborn way and kept them alive for ten bitter years.

Until they died on him.

The grass survives. Dad waters it four times a week, at night, to save on water. He stands with the red hose and directs it carefully, apportioning the stream correctly and justly. He won't put a sprinkler in the yard, just as he won't bring a television set into the house. Alone, lit by a pale triangle of light from the porch, he waters the heavy soil, and a feeling of creativity comes over him.

His son up and left for America, but the grass stayed behind, helpless and faithful and still turning green from year to year despite the fact that the son's return looks ever more doubtful.

If there is bad news, Mom hides it at the end, toward the close of the letter, to soften the blow. "Nimrod's grandfather had a heart attack but now he's OK." I lift my gaze to the top of the mountain out the window. I always loved Nimrod's grandfather, not having had a grandfather of my own. And now, go figure what happened to him and when. Mom, in her efforts to send me a healthy and pleasant picture from Israel, won't provide more detail. At the end of the page, her handwriting is strong and optimistic, and she describes, in her traditional paragraph, the approach of spring.

And then comes Dad, in strong letters drawn with strokes that tail off as if refusing to quit. He corrects Mom's predictions of the weather in the appropriate places, grumbles about work, and signs off with the standard line: "And all the rest Mom has already written." Sometimes he plants a solitary island of emotion: "We thought about you today" or even "We miss you," always in the plural.

This time there is also a P.S.: "We thought we might possibly come to visit you in December, if it works out."

I put the letter down in shock. A parental visit in Moab, Utah! For a moment I try to imagine them entering the rusty gate and struggling with the screen door, but I can't.

Again I read the letter. We thought we might possibly come to visit you in December, if it works out. Three qualifiers in one sentence. It wasn't money or distance or health that dictated those qualifiers. It was our tense relationship, layers of trepidation and pain, suspicion and grievance, untranslated love and years of frustration. Through all that, they don't have a clue if I want them to come, and neither do I.

Since the letter, I haven't been able to see a single thing without thinking, What will they say?

My room, for example.

A rug and a wicker table and an old armchair and two posters of landscapes, one of nearby Arches National Park and the second of the Banyas River back home.

Dad will ask why I don't buy myself a desk.

In my room I lie down and listen to Joni Mitchell, whose sad notes make my autumn depression a little sweeter. With her I manage to see outside myself, to boundless blue vistas, into her longing.

Mom would hear ten seconds of this song and say, Why is she yelling, this woman? I close my eyes and listen to the cassette. The words, in a language not my own, don't connect, but the syllables have a life of their own, hovering in space, abstract.

Now the song I love. It calms me enough that my mind wanders, only to return with the next song. And not alone, but with a guy, pleasing and fair, who lies down in my bed and dreams my dreams with me.

Dad will ask, Do you have a girlfriend yet, and I will smile with difficulty and tell him no, and Mom will stare at him and at me with a confused look, a look both accused and accusing. And we will never go further.

In the evening, I'll go to Betsy's for a cup of tea. Betsy is almost seventy-seven, and she has acres of curly hair and a porch with three chairs upholstered in yellow where she sits and looks back on her life. She and I have nothing in common aside from this tea and her memory, which, sparked by my curiosity, takes off, flutters about, and alights in the least expected places, and then her face softens as if returning to a former self. The porch darkens and a reddish-blue band of light descends on the rock that looks like a giant bird. Only then does Betsy make the tea and lay out dinner for me. On her table the stories pile up, suffused with a desert aroma.

Mom will say, What business do you have with this old lady who could be your grandmother?

And then I will have to explain to them what I'm doing here.

I won't tell everything. I'm not sure that I understand, myself. I'll show them the flyers about rafting. I'll take them to the cabin on the banks of the Colorado River. I'll introduce them to old Donald, who hired me to work on the boats three years ago, when I happened on this place during a cross-country trip. He'll murmur something and they'll murmur back in Hebrew.

Everything I say will sound unconvincing, as if there were no breaking the wall of their doubt and mistrust, and under Dad's demanding gaze I will shrink and shrink, and in the end nothing will remain of me but a small bubble of apology, a crumb, then nothing.

At six I get up to clean the room. At this blessed hour the specks of dust have a special radiance, but Mom and dust are ancient enemies, and I mobilize against it with her methods, which don't help but only bestow on it another, almost spiritual quality. I know that Mom won't accept graciously that dust has any qualities. Without looking at me and with an iron hand, she'll chase away the specks that have escaped and will leave my room pure and clean.

With the good morning sun, I hang a sign in the entrance, "Welcome Mom and Dad." Three times I move the flowers, trying to give my hovel the appearance of a home. The pink carnations look a little confused.

Next to the bed I put two maps of the area and pause for a moment. Mom and Dad in my bed in Utah. I think of them in the old bed in Holon. I remember playing between them on Saturday mornings. I can't imagine them in my bed, and I go outside where the sun has grown stronger.

Why look at this as a nightmare, I demand of myself. And from the pain headquarters, I send out the order not to be angry, only to love, for a week, anyway.

I turn the vase so the flowers will enjoy the glow of the desert, and it's as if I'm offended in advance by the thought that Mom and Dad won't even notice them. I put them back.

It's not that I don't want to write; it just doesn't work for me. You know that I don't write. Even from the army I didn't write to you. If I had money I would call. I know that you understand, but I'm just explaining.

And also, what am I going to write? About the boats? About the weather? I have nothing to write.

I actually tried to start a few times. Just a couple of months ago, when I got the letter that you were coming, I sat an entire evening where Mom is sitting now and I tried to write. But nothing came out. Writing is not my thing. What can I do?

I look at the flowers, and they don't answer me. In vain, I rehearse dialogues of things I'll never say.

When they come, they are waiting for me (I'm late) on the light blue plastic chairs under the "Arrivals" sign, pale and worried. Even when I reach them the worry doesn't go away. Because this worry goes all the way back to Abraham, the first father, and no reasoning is going to uproot it. In Steve's Café, two days later, Dad drums with his fork on the table and casually asks, Nu, what's with the girls here, and Mom surprises me: apparently prepared for this moment, she says, Moshek, don't ask too much. When he has something to announce, he'll say so. And Dad, not pleased with the interruption, throws her a look, glances down at his fork, drums a bit more and concludes: Yes, yes. Yes, yes.

When it's all over, the moment of parting arrives at the place where the baggage carts are parked. We don't say anything important, worn out by each other but not wanting to take leave of each other, stuck in a fixed trap. The tears burst out at the end, after they've disappeared with the last of the travelers at the gate, pale and old, and a last wave good-bye has died in the closing door of the elevator, and then, to the roar of the engines warming up, I understand that we can only be close when we're far apart.

> Dear Oren,
> We got back three days ago, and, as usual after trips, we're asking ourselves if we were really in America. It was a little warm on Monday, but when we saw Miri and Gili, we forgot everything. They made us open the suitcases before we even left the airport (by the way, they've changed the whole arrangement at the airport, you wouldn't recognize

it at all). Gili is happy with the sneakers despite the fact that they are a tiny bit big on him.

The yard wasn't in the best condition. Your brother said he'd watered it, but Dad will have to work hard to get the grass back in shape. On Saturday the whole family is coming, and also Menachem from Hadera. It seems to me he hasn't been here for two years, since the last Seder we made, that you weren't at. And Naphtali and Ella may come too. We hope we'll have the slides from the trip back by then. Other than that, there's nothing new. Look after yourself, and buy yourself a sweater like we said.

Kisses,
Mom

Shalom Oren,

Mom has written everything there is to tell. The yard will be all right. With a little effort and some late winter rain everything will be back to normal. I'm attaching a few articles about the political situation. If you like we'll get you a subscription to the newspaper, so you'll know what's going on.

Kisses,
Dad

It's turned cool. I ride my bike along the banks of the river and turn onto Highway 55. My eyes are fixed on the white stripe at the edge, focused so hard that I don't realize it's getting dark.

Suddenly I think about Mom. How much I would like to sit with her on the porch and eat grapes.

Highway 55 forks. There is something relaxing in this well-numbered, well-marked system, and it gives you the illusion that you know where you're going.

In the fading light I turn onto a road that isn't numbered. I strain my muscles, cut through air and water, gather every possible longing into the basket on the front of my bike, strengthen my grip on the handlebars, suck air into my cheeks and blow it out, and while my legs keep up their pedaling, I am wrapped in fog and glide through it with the confidence of being on automatic pilot. I feel the chill and the salty mist. My eyes close for a second, and in my head a tune plays from my childhood. I emerge from the gray into the roundabout at the entrance to the town, and my tired legs accelerate one last time, and in this way I slip into our yard, almost falling over the red hose Dad is using to water in the dark, and I drop the bike against the porch steps. Inside, Mom is reading the newspaper, and she raises her eyes and studies me with simple affection, not surprised, and I lay my head on her bosom and say almost voicelessly, "Now it's all right, it's all right now."

And she caresses me and nods her head.

Lilly

Translated by Chana Jenny Weisberg

Where HaLamed Heh Street bends around and Judges Street rises to meet it, the presence of a small café on that corner is a mystery to all. It has already been there for so many years, however, that it is impossible to imagine the neighborhood without it. The owner is Mordechai, a silent man, with a constant smile fixed on his face—sometimes sweet, sometimes cynical, sometimes both. At his side is Lilly, everybody's sweetheart. Around her the café keeps on ticking, with quiet efficiency and wonderful order.

Despite the crowded space and the lack of sophistication, as well as the questionable taste of the coffee, the place has earned such popularity that it is difficult to get a table. For that reason, truly strange coalitions come about, in the form of two strangers sharing a table and exchanging opinions about the morning news in the complimentary newspapers that Mordechai gives out with the coffee. There are stories of two married couples who started out this way, as well as business partners, and of course, several of the city's juiciest tales of adultery.

The routine of the café has never changed. At six thirty, tops quarter of seven, Mordechai arrives on his motorcycle wearing a shabby gray coat and carrying a plastic briefcase. Achmed, the dishwasher, is already there. They open the three locks—one of which always gives them trouble. A few minutes later, after Achmed has finished taking the chairs down from the tables, Judge P. hobbles in leaning heavily on his cane, ready for his latte. Achmed then goes to get the newspapers and almost always returns in time for Judge P. to read his favorite column along with his first latte of the day. Within fifteen minutes, the three regulars of the morning arrive and grab their tables. At seven thirty, Lilly makes her entrance and brings with her a quality that is difficult to explain—spiritual and physical all at once. By eight o'clock not a table is free, and wordlessly Lilly floats between them while serving the regulars their drinks and pastries. At the same time, and with the same ease, she gives the others the sense that they belong. Along with the morning pastries the patrons digest the morning news, and at times from one of the corner tables a conversation breaks out that sweeps around and envelops the whole café.

Besides the art collector Odelya Etrogi, who comes from Revisionist roots, and maybe one or two others, the orientation of the café is center-left. Because of this, the conversations proceed in a generally predictable direction, and the opinions expressed suspiciously match some of the articles that appear in the morning papers.

One morning, not long ago, Lilly did not arrive. At seven thirty, expectant glances rose to the door. The regulars waited with a certain irritation, but still she did not come. Mordechai called her, but there was no answer. The smile which usually sat on his face disappeared: he was worried about her, and what's more, he realized that he was stuck and would have to do everything alone. Luckily, it turned out that in addition to washing dishes and cleaning tables, Achmed also knew how to make coffee—even though no one had ever taught him.

Everyone had a different response to the event. There were some people who absolutely refused to eat their pastries until Lilly arrived. Mr. M. from TV, for example, waited and waited, and finally he left without drinking anything. Odelya Etrogi said that her whole day was ruined. They all sat that way for a long time, facing the door. They came up with all sorts of hypotheses. Maybe something happened in her family? Maybe she had lost track of time while at a party, and not gotten home until terribly late? All sorts of things like that. Suddenly they saw that they did not know a thing about her. They only knew one thing—that she made their day. They realized that they did not come because of the coffee or for the almost-fresh pastry, but rather, completely and totally because of her. They came because of her shadow of a smile, and the confidence she gave them, and because she knew better than anyone how they love their mornings—instant coffee and after that a poppy-seed croissant, along with the inside section of *Haaretz*. Everyone and their habits.

They sat that way for a long time, with eyes hanging on the door, confused, worried, longing. Whoever left, went silently. Judge P. left a telephone number, so they could call and tell him what happened. Ron the student skipped his morning classes, and in the end he stayed the whole day. By the end of the day, Mordechai simply threw him out because he always closes at eight thirty, tops quarter of nine.

Afterward, Mordechai did not tell anyone what had happened, besides the fact that Lilly was healthy and well, but "not working with us anymore." The next day there was a new hardworking waitress named Arianna, who had her strong points, but she was no Lilly. And after her, Meirav, and Orna, and Sigalit, and Shosh. Each one lasted a week or two, not more.

That whole period, Lilly remained the topic of choice at the café. While Mordechai kept his lips sealed, wild theories circulated about what had happened. They said that she had decided to open up a competing café on the other side of the city, and they also said that she had been having a romance with Mordechai, and that they had had a fight. In came Odelya Etrogi one morning with a story that Lilly had joined some sort of Messianic cult and that she would soon fly to Colombia to live in a monastery in the mountains.

The truth, fortunately, was much less dramatic. It came to light quickly, since the city is small, and everyone, after all, knows everyone else, and they also meet them on the street. What happened was that Lilly went to take her driver's test. She claimed that she had told Mordechai two weeks before, but he doesn't remember anything. He, for his part, was not willing to forgive what seemed to him critical damage to the workplace and irresponsibility of the first degree.

When these facts were known, there was some talk in the café that maybe it was possible to mend what had been torn apart. The regulars created a pressure group. Judge P. was appointed as the go-between, and he suggested that Lilly should apologize and Mordechai would take her back. But the matter was not so simple. Lilly refused to apologize and Mordechai refused to give in.

When they saw there was no choice, they decided to go all the way, and stopped coming. It was pretty sad to see Mordechai reading a newspaper on his own, sitting with nothing to do the whole day except make up jobs for Achmed. When he ran out of ideas, he let Achmed sit down, and then it turned out that Achmed could read, and that he preferred *Maariv*. It seems that they had several heart-to-heart talks at that time. At any rate, it did not take Mordechai much time to understand that if he wanted to make a living, he would have to bring Lilly back.

In the end it was Mordechai who apologized, and also gave in, and also raised her salary, and even visited her home three times until she agreed.

Luckily, when the riots started up again in the Territories, life had returned to normal. Once again there was somewhere to conduct the morning symposium, and to be comforted about the headlines over pastries as before. And the main thing, Lilly was there—as tranquil as always, mixing into the coffee cups the feeling that life is not so bitter, after all.

That Boy

Translated by Charlie Buckholtz

For a long time now, I have been going to the bar once a week. Without excitement or expectation—more like someone going to work. Dutifully I drink, trade glances, flirt a little and drink more, and then, if I'm lucky, they come home with me. I hate going with them. You never know what you'll find. A desolate fridge, that's what you'll find, and then you can't get it up. How excited can you be when there's nothing in the fridge?

Yesterday I didn't want to go. When I got home from the gym, I said to myself, forget it, go to bed, you're not alone there, you have the TV. But nothing was on. Seinfeld had a lame new girlfriend, Channel 2 was an annoying romance, and the Nature Channel was showing mating rituals of turtles. *Enough.*

I shaved, put on tons of aftershave, and combed my hair for ten minutes. I have flowing, silver hair. It's been that way from a young age, not white but silver, and because of this distinctness I invest time in an appropriate hairdo. I do it myself; I don't let anybody touch my hair.

At the entrance to the bar were a bunch of all-too-familiar characters whom I ignored. What can you do in a country this small, where after a while you more or less know everyone and can divide them into two groups, those you've slept with and those you haven't?

Dikman, the hot bartender, was there. It helps when he's there. When you don't have anybody to talk with, you can always chat with him, though "chat" is a big word for what we do.

"How ya doin', Dikman?"

"Not bad, not bad. What about you, everything's good?"

"I need some fresh air. Are you painting?"

"Who has time?"

He paints, Dikman, he may go to Bezalel art school. He's shocked I remember. Of course I remember. I remember everything he says. But he is, as it were, way out of my league: Dikman sleeps with the gods.

I killed an hour or two. There was nothing happening from any angle. The music was terrible. I can tolerate all different kinds of music, but theirs, I don't know where they find it. And of course you have to make like it's cool and nod your head to the beat.

I couldn't decide whether to have another drink or admit defeat and leave. There was a slight chance of answering the glance of someone who'd been staring at me a long time from the other side of the bar, who I wasn't into at all. I decided to ignore him. How much can a person compromise?

A little while later, an older guy sat down next to me, maybe forty, but he looked good in a purple shirt, a green jacket. In principle I have no problem with older guys, as long as they look really, really good. Not that I don't prefer young guys. But if there's an older guy who really, *really* looks good . . .

He sat next to me, ordered a drink, seemed confident enough. Said hi to the person on the other side of him and also to me. He had a natural way of connecting, as if this wasn't a gay bar and relationships between people were not complicated at all. I offered him a cigarette and he turned it down. He said smoke bothers him. A strange thing to say in a bar, but that's what he said.

We started talking. He asked me about myself. I didn't answer; I don't like talking about myself. I never know where to begin. Someone you meet in a bar—what can you really tell him? The only thing that comes easy is work, people talk about what they do, but what I do is somewhat classified, as they say; so what does that leave?

He talked about himself, freely, as if he knew me. He talked about the boyfriend he'd had. For fifteen years he had an Australian boyfriend who died of AIDS. They lived abroad in all kinds of places. He mentioned many beautiful cities; it sounded not bad at all. He spoke about his boyfriend without sadness, like he was still around and just happened to be traveling. Obviously my first thought was that if his boyfriend had AIDS he probably also has it, but anyway at that point I had written off sex, there was too much talk. That's how it is with me. Somebody talks to me for more than three minutes, I lose interest. After that it's like sleeping with your cousin.

He said his name was Danny. So be it. Danny is usually the first name someone will come up with off the top of their head. I am also frequently Danny. But lately I'm Alon. The last few weeks on the Internet I've been Liron, which to me is a young-sounding name. Not long ago I had a one-night stand with a Liron, age sixteen.

"Danny" told me he was a cellist. He was always at concerts. Again he tossed off ten beautiful cities in half a minute. It made me really want to travel; too bad there's nobody to go with. From the time his parents died he almost never came to Israel, just when they invited him for concerts with the Philharmonic, that kind of thing. I got from all this that he was important in the classical music world, but he wasn't arrogant about it—not at all. I ordered another round for both of us. Dikman knows what I like and how I like it, and he took good care of the musician too. I asked him why the cello, admitting it's an instrument I know little about, even how many strings it has. At least I knew it has strings.

"The cello was coincidental enough. My mother brought me to the neighborhood conservatory. We lived in Kiryat Hayim. Anyone who played seriously commuted to Haifa. But I was seven years old and I had never played anything, and my mother certainly never thought anything would come of it." His face was like a round, smiling melon, and I felt comfortable, which almost never happens; I smiled, too.

I didn't know I was smiling until I looked in the mirror. The whole wall behind the bar is a big mirror, where I check my hair periodically to see if anything has come suddenly undone. I looked at myself and then at him, at his fingers, which were long and strong, a cellist's tools. Fingers are a very male appendage, I think. He touched the cup, then relaxed, touched and relaxed, touching on different memories. "When you ask a music teacher which instrument they recommend, 90 percent of the answer depends on what teacher is available. That's how it was with me. The director put a guitar in my hand, a violin, a clarinet, whatever they had, and asked if any of them appealed to me. I said the guitar, but I wasn't sure. I didn't have self-confidence, I didn't even know if I wanted to play at all. She sized me up and said it seemed to her the cello; and that coincidentally a new cello teacher had arrived, who might be able to take me on if he had any room."

And then, from nowhere, I remembered that I had heard this story before. And I remembered when. It had been at least twenty years.

My mother and I are sitting on the two big heavy American armchairs watching TV. Father is in his office, working on bills. He is always working on bills. Mother caresses the right arm of the chair, her foot on the round ottoman with the worn upholstery. The light from the television flickers on the wall above the piano. Mother holds her glasses in her hand. Sometimes she wears them, but usually not. We don't speak. Even when there are musical performances between programs or long monotonous public service announcements, we don't speak. She's already asked if I finished my homework, and apparently I said yes, otherwise she would be nagging me. Sometimes she says something to the television, one or two words, "Yes" or "Disgusting" or "*Look* at them," in her deep cigarette voice.

The host prattles on, followed by some musical segment. Mostly I'm not watching; I'm dreaming. I have strange dreams. In my dreams I'm a king, or a pilot, or a king who is also a pilot. It goes without saying that no one knows of my dreams. There's no one to talk to, left, right, or center; I walk completely alone through this impossible childhood.

The music finishes, and now you see the host. He has a long, slanted face and lots of hair. This was the style back then. His hair looks like he just left the beauty parlor. The camera zooms out, and slowly you see who's sitting next to him. A cultural discussion ensues, horribly boring, like always on these shows.

Suddenly there is an unexplained tension. Mother stops caressing the armchair and puts on her glasses. I don't look at her, but I know that her eyebrows are squinched tight. I want to leave, but it would be suspicious to go to my room right now. Also, I have nothing else to do. Television is all there is, and television is only one channel and the whole country is sitting and watching it. From father's office, the slow ticking of the typewriter. Father is the slowest typist in the world. I play with my toes. I have a talent that no one else has: I can touch any toe to any other toe, even the big toe to the pinkie on each foot. If I do it for more than a few seconds my mother gets annoyed; she says it stunts the foot's growth. But now she doesn't say anything; she moves a little closer to the television, which is already pretty close, and watches the screen with a kind of hostility.

"And why don't you live in Israel?" asks the coiffed host.

"Obviously I have my career in the symphony," says the interviewee.

"And is that the *only* reason?" wonders the host, who clearly knows something we don't.

I move the two far toes of my right foot toward each other, then the two of my left. I haven't yet managed to do both feet at the same time.

"No, there is another reason," the cellist says, and suddenly I feel so much tension in the room that I think maybe, yes, I will go to my room; but I don't make it in time.

"There is also the fact that I live there with my boyfriend."

Mother smacks the arm of her chair and says, *"I knew it,"* with controlled fury. I hold my breath and for the first time touch both sets of toes together. She gets up from the television and goes to the kitchen.

He asked me if I was okay, did I need a handkerchief. I didn't say anything. It's weird that he goes around with a handkerchief; I thought there weren't people like that anymore. I preferred a napkin from the bar. He looked to the side; he knew he wasn't supposed to look at me like that.

I asked if he had ever been on television. He said he's on a lot. I said I thought I remembered him from some talk show, many years ago. He was shocked I remembered. "I've changed a lot since then." I couldn't tell if he'd changed or not because I didn't remember him at all, his voice, nothing, all I remembered was how my mother went completely silent, and the host continued to blah blah blah with no idea of what was going on in our home. Despite the fact that I've seen him a million times since then, I never connected him to that night, although—and I don't know if this is related—I always get a strange feeling when he comes on. He's still there on Channel 1, with a few other heroes from those days: an extra pound here, a gray hair there, but their voices haven't changed, and they're watching, all the time, what I've become and what I haven't become since.

I suggested we leave. I told him the truth—that it wasn't for sex but to talk. It was a little weird to say it, because no one likes hearing you don't want to have sex with them. But there was a closeness, and I didn't want it to end. He told me how hard it was for him since his boyfriend died. His boyfriend returns to him in dreams, he said, sends warmth, guidance, signs.

Danny (it turned out that this actually was his name) invited me to his hotel. I agreed. Dikman said bye. You can never tell with him if he notices whether you leave the bar alone or with someone. I would've been happy if he cared a little. I would've been happy if anyone cared a little.

We went to the hotel and sat out on the balcony, each with a drink. It was a little hot until we started to get a nice breeze from the sea. At first we didn't speak, but then I felt I needed to tell him, which is rare with me. I don't understand people who right away tell their most personal things.

I told him about that time with my mother. He gave the impression he understood, even though I didn't really explain it. After all, she didn't do anything, she just said, "I knew it." He nodded, and then asked how my parents responded when I told them.

"I didn't exactly tell them."

"Meaning?"

"My father I never told anything. My father is not the kind of person that's, you know, approachable."

"And your mother?"

"With my mother it wasn't clear."

"What wasn't clear?"

I took a deep breath. I myself don't know if I understand this thing. I just never really got around to telling anyone.

"Once I tried to tell her. Actually, I said it pretty clearly."

"What did you say?"

"That I'm not attracted to women."

"And what did she say?"

"She didn't say anything."

"Then what did you do?"

"I said it again, and then I started to tell her some other things."

"What things?"

"I don't remember exactly. That there's a guy I really love, something like that."

"And what did she say?"

"Nothing."

"What happened afterward?"

"Nothing. I left. For a long time I thought maybe she was thinking about something else at that moment, and didn't notice what I said. I've never been sure of what she knew and what she didn't."

He brought his hand close to me, almost touching. It was clear this was exactly the line—not a centimeter more.

Nothing happened. We went inside and listened to jazz until very late. We didn't speak. We slept, three feet apart, fully dressed. And I thought of my mother, who died a long time ago. She doesn't return to me in dreams. Or maybe it's just that I don't return to her.

I looked at Danny, asleep. I hoped his dead boyfriend would come and visit him.

I recalled a fantasy from my childhood. I wanted to have a really good friend, who I could do anything with: go to the beach, trade stamps, fly airplanes, laugh, hit, eat meals his mom would make. I looked at Danny, and I thought that sleeping he kind of looks like a little boy, and that he could have been that boy who never came.

Sushi

Translated by Ken Frieden

There's an act I have that goes like this: I come in with a suitcase, climb onto the stage, and ask the audience what's in the suitcase.

—Bread, someone says.
—*No.*
—A camera.
—*No.*
—Money.
—*You, out there, in the back?*
—A hand grenade. (*The audience laughs.*)
—*No. You?*
—A book of poems.
—*No.*

When they get to the point that they're dying of curiosity, I reach into the suitcase and pull out my ego. The audience is stunned. This they didn't expect. Then we do our bit with a tango. My ego is dressed in a coat of many colors and a fur hat, while I'm wearing a black body suit. The audience goes crazy and begs for more. The curtain comes down. The curtain rises. My ego bows first and I, hesitantly, after him. As far as I'm concerned, that's enough, but he announces:

—*And now, the pas de deux.* (We dance it to perfection. He shows them everything he's got, wiggling enthusiastically, with unusual panache.)

Shy as I am, the only way for me to get through this is by going into a frenzy, as if I were dancing to save my life. That's why it turns out so well. Finally I say that, if they want, they can ask us questions. But they just shout:

—More, more!

We don't have any more, I say, do you have questions?

They're not interested in anything. At that point, neither am I. So I put my ego back into the suitcase. If we're lucky they give us a check (postdated by a year or two), but often they don't pay us at all and don't even thank us. Afterward, when we're alone, our big argument begins.

I tell my ego, Come on, let's go home and eat. He wants to go to a restaurant. I tell him okay, let's go to my girlfriend's house—she's a great cook. He doesn't say anything. She really does give us a feast, but he's not satisfied. When we leave her house, he wants me to take him to Japan because he's dying for sushi. No matter what I say he goes on wailing, Japan! To Japan! I yell at him, Dwarf! You dwarf! Finally I agree to take him to a cheap falafel stand on the condition that he'll give me some peace. He promises, but as soon as we leave the place he starts to whine:

—*All I really wanted was sushi!*

Tuesday and
Thursday Mornings

Translated by Naomi Seidman

One Tuesday morning, the passersby on Emek Refaim Street were surprised by an unusual sight: a red-haired youth, wearing a green silk garment, had set down a portable cassette player at a corner of the street where it intersected with one of the side roads that led to the railroad tracks. To the notes of mystical music, rich with bells and a harp, he twisted his body in soft, rhythmic movements. His eyes were shut, and his entire being radiated focus and attention.

After a while he bent toward a brown blanket he had spread beneath him, kneeled on the ground, and picked up the beat again, placing his hands by his sides, moving them this way and that, lifting them into the air. Very slowly the dancer turned into a flower about to awaken, about to bloom. His body became a stalk, his hands leaves, and from his shirt he unrolled a high, purplish collar, which covered half his head, and over it his red hair cascaded, long and smooth, like a beautiful, fresh blossom.

The small crowd cheered enthusiastically. One man said it reminded him of birth: so exciting, so true, so harmonious. A flower had come into the world.

Only then did the young man open his eyes, which were blue as pools of water, and look around himself with interest. From his backpack he drew out a cap, set it down on the blanket, and soon picked it up again, now filled with coins.

When they tried to get him to talk, he said only that he was a tourist and that his name was Pascal, and then he shut off with a shy smile. He even turned down, with a sweet gesture of gratitude and apology, the cup of coffee offered by Zehava from the corner café, who had been watching in amazement with her morning customers. Within a few minutes he had disappeared with his handful of props in the direction of downtown, leaving a trail of admirers.

On Thursday he was there again. The crowd had grown. This time Zehava wanted him off the corner. She thought that if this was going to be a regular act, it would impede the foot traffic into her café. Fortunately, a few regulars managed to persuade her to let him continue.

The sight of the blossoming flower aroused just as much excitement this time, and even more coins filled the cap. Pascal responded to the rhythmic applause with an encore. From the folds of his cloak he unfurled colorfully segmented cloths, which his wide-stretched arms formed into wings, and dancing gaily and rhythmically he was transformed into a multicolored butterfly fluttering among the flowers.

On the Tuesday after that the encore turned into a whole separate performance, and Pascal fluttered among the spectators, who had become more numerous, sipping nectar from their stamen-hair, resting for a moment on a bough-shoulder. Just as the blossoming flower had done, the butterfly succeeded in penetrating the hearts of these Jerusalemites. One girl who had hosted the redhead on her shoulder for a long moment was so moved that her eyes welled up. An older man murmured, "A true artist. A totally true artist." The applause continued for a long time.

Tuesday and Thursday mornings on Emek Refaim took on a special quality. Pascal would arrive just before eleven, spread out his blanket among the fans that had already gathered in anticipation, pull on his long cloak, and open the show with the blossoming flower. After the cap had been filled once or twice, he would get something to eat at Zehava's, who in the meantime had come to recognize his commercial value and had even persuaded him to accept a free meal.

And so Pascal would arrive for the second half of his program well-fed and satisfied, and he would embody the butterfly with fascinating ease, each time choosing three lucky flowers. What had begun as just a brief stopover on some chance shoulder soon developed into a powerful artistic flirtation. He would rest his red mane in the curve of the chosen neck, encircle the person once or twice, and finally draw them into a dance. Once, when the spectators were particularly fired up, the butterfly number turned into a mass dance that swept up everyone passing by, and which stopped traffic on busy Emek Refaim for a full ten minutes.

The butterfly, even more than the flower, touched something deep in people's souls. The presence of Pascal so close quickened the breath. Swarms of butterflies arose within one's soul, fluttering in one's body and bursting into the world. After that, one felt strangely light, as if a tangle of emotion had suddenly come undone, been set free.

With the success of his street performance, Pascal also began to open up a bit. For the first time he started to exchange a few words with the crowd, brief and modest.

He revealed that he was from Luxembourg, that he was twenty-six years old, and that the previous stop on his long journey, which was of course both spiritual and geographic, had been Spain. Although he wasn't religious, he had always been drawn to the Holy Land and to Jerusalem. There was something special that had called him specifically to this spot, to the German Colony and to Emek Refaim Street, something he couldn't describe.

These few words made an enormous impression on the circle of admirers. What especially excited them was the fact that, of all the places in the world, this gifted young man had chosen their little corner, which until then had appeared dull and mundane, but which now had been magically transformed into a wellspring of butterflies.

The owners of other cafés on the street tried to bribe Pascal into moving his performance closer to them. Zehava rooted out these devious schemes and opened a full-fledged assault. On one front she spruced up her menu and invited him to eat at her place twice more each day (an invitation which he shyly accepted), and on the other front she gave her rivals such a talking-to that they backed off in fright. Just to be safe she also ostentatiously dropped fifties and sometimes even hundred-shekel notes into the cap, which was starting to come apart at the seams. Pascal would look embarrassed at the gesture. In general, anything related to money made him uneasy, as if the material world were more than he could bear.

The first person who managed to penetrate his defenses was actually Uzi Peled, a young architect from the Sherman and Pesach firm. He and his colleagues at the office timed their lunch breaks according to Pascal's performances, which had become the most important part of their day. To the annoyance of their employers Sherman and Pesach, these lunch breaks were growing longer, with the junior architects standing around with the draftswomen and secretaries and speculating on the personality and sexual orientation of the fascinating redhead who danced among them twice a week on the sidewalks of Emek Refaim.

Uzi Peled, who was himself an introverted and shy type, gathered his courage and began the conversation. The two found a common language and spent an evening over beers, for which Uzi Peled insisted on paying. He learned that the artist had left behind a brokenhearted girlfriend in Luxembourg. His own heart had also broken, but there was no choice: he had had to leave on his journey. All this he relayed charmingly enough in French-accented English, but he refused to go into further detail. Instead he insisted on hearing the story of Uzi Peled's life. This story struck him as fascinating, although to the architect it seemed that, aside from his military duty with the combat engineering unit, the details of which he had difficulty conveying in English, nothing of any note had ever happened to him.

At the end of the pleasant evening, Uzi Peled wondered where his conversational partner was staying now. Pascal acknowledged that he had no place of his own other than a bed in a crowded dormitory at one of the hostels in the Old City. Right on the spot, Uzi Peled invited him to stay with him, in the guest bedroom of his Baka apartment.

Pascal said that the generous offer was far beyond what he could allow himself to accept. He would be happy to pay, but there was no way he could do that at the moment.

Whatever money he was making at the performances had to be saved for the remainder of his journey.

"It's not about the money," the Israeli declared, insulted. "You'll be my guest! It's an honor for me, please understand!" At the end of it all, not without a struggle and not without the help of another bottle of beer, an understanding was reached: The artist would pack up his things that very night, and Uzi Peled would drive him and his possessions from the hostel near Jaffa Gate to Baka. Peled even took the trouble to help him carry his backpack. They didn't stop to pay up, since Pascal—as he explained—had already paid in advance for the week.

During the time that Pascal was staying with him, Uzi Peled felt his spirits lift. It was true that they spent most of their time together watching television, but even this was a change of the host's routine. Pascal knew no one in Israel, and so had no social life. In fact, Uzi Peled also had no one to invite over or who would invite him over in turn. He felt a little guilty: his guest deserved better than this wasteland. Once when he came home from work and heard Pascal talking on the telephone, he was relieved: Maybe he had already made some new acquaintances here, and if he had, he might stay on a few more weeks.

Uzi Peled was disappointed, then, when Pascal thanked him at the end of the week and told him he was moving on, to some other place. "I don't want to impose," he said, more than once, and even when Uzi Peled promised him repeatedly that he wasn't imposing, on the contrary, the artist insisted on thanking him and leaving.

The other place was the dark apartment of Irena, a student in the theater department, who was among the more enthusiastic spectators on Tuesdays and Thursdays. When he moved in with her with his few possessions, Irena was happier than she had ever been in her life. She prepared a romantic supper for him, with beautifully spiced dishes, incense and candles. At first Pascal was quiet, although when she spoke he listened willingly enough. For her part, she told him about her previous boyfriend and, when she had loosened up a bit, also about the boyfriend before that. By the time they had gone through a bottle of red wine, at least six other previous boyfriends had come and gone. Normally she had a tendency to go into the most intimate details, but her guest didn't seem too enthusiastic when the conversation went in that direction.

Irena felt compelled to keep talking with him. His blue eyes excited her, and his willingness to listen and encourage her lent strength to the sublime feelings he aroused in her. But at the same time, even though it seemed clear that in his own quiet way he was interested in her, she decided not to press. At the end of the enchanting evening, as the two of them floated gently on clouds of a certain herb that grew on her windowsill, she persuaded him to take her comfortable bed and spread out an improvised bedroll for herself in the kitchen.

In the days that followed, the shy stranger continued to captivate her, seemingly against his will. The more he tried to stay out of her way, the more drawn she felt to his graceful movements, his modesty, his broad horizons. To her surprise, nothing happened between them. She sensed that he was interested in her, but their conversations late into the night never turned into anything more. And she, who had experience in such matters, held off at this stage from taking the initiative. She did everything possible short of touching him: she pressed him to borrow her car in order to get to know Israel, took him out to restaurants far beyond her modest budget, and introduced him, with characteristic openness, to a host of friends of both sexes—all of them bohemian types as good-hearted as he himself was.

It didn't surprise her in the least that he found common ground with each of them, and most of them became his friends, too. In her heart she wavered between the hope that her friends, whom she saw as her true achievement, would help him recognize her deepest qualities and lead him to reveal the feelings for her she so longed for, and the dread that some other woman from the fascinating world she was opening before him would make a move and leave her, wounded, far behind.

What actually happened was different from either of those possibilities. Pascal showed a powerful intellectual interest in a long series of friends and friends of friends that Irena presented to him. In his social life, which had suddenly blossomed, the youth with the eyes like pools was just as wonderfully charismatic as he had been in his performances on Emek Refaim. He could talk about (or, even more so, listen to others talk about) philosophy, art, technology, and even Jewish history.

Irena's friends found in Pascal a conversation partner who was fascinating and attractive—especially attractive. In the short month since he had first appeared on the scene, at least ten young men and women were ready to do whatever it took to fall into bed with him. Each and every one of them spent many hours in conversation with him, but from all appearances, no one got further than talk. There was something so spiritual in him that any contact with the material world could only spoil things. He was like a beautiful, high-flying bird. There was no point in trying to catch such a bird—it was born for freedom, for the heights, for the great open spaces.

Irena, caught between frustration and incomprehension, wondered about the true reason for the screen of words that her guest had erected between the two of them, and between himself and the rest of the world. She did not believe in human gods. A physiological, sexual, or psychological explanation of this incapacity seemed much more reasonable to her. She began to feel sorry for the young man. So much talent, so much emotion, so much beauty, but when one got to the bottom line, nothing. Nada.

She was prepared to do a lot to help him, and even made some secret (and very expensive) plans in this direction. But then something terrible happened to her that sent her in a completely different direction.

She lost all her money.

She couldn't remember how it happened. One morning she was looking for her money, but it wasn't there, and it also wasn't there, and also wasn't there. If not for Pascal, who was there and who helped her to organize her thinking and stay logical, she would have gone out of her mind. In one blow she had lost her meager savings, and there was nothing she could do about it. For three days she retraced her steps again and again. She wasn't an organized person. She wasn't even sure exactly how much money she had had, maybe a couple of thousand. And it was her whole nest egg, everything she had in the world.

The thought that Pascal himself could be a suspect wouldn't have occurred to her if he hadn't suddenly disappeared. It was, coincidentally, a Tuesday, and she found herself drifting like a sleepwalker down to the corner on Emek Refaim. Along with dozens of his fans she waited and waited, tears clogging her throat. His willowy figure and red crown did not appear. On Thursday she waited again, still refusing to come to terms with the bitter facts that were beginning to come into focus for her. That same day a long-faced young man came up to her and asked if she was the one who had taken Pascal in. His name, Uzi Peled, was written on the telephone bill he showed her. The sum displayed at the bottom of the bill was 8,866 shekels. The shock Irena felt as she looked at the bill was almost equal to what she felt two weeks later when, stupefied, she looked over her own bill, which had soared to almost ten thousand shekels. The itemized statement listed countries all over the world that someone had called from her telephone. With every new day she discovered, with mounting anxiety, something else missing from her apartment (jewelry she had inherited when her mother died, a rare book in German, and so forth).

Even worse: Her good friends, who had also been privileged to host her exotic artist, began to report the disappearance of their own money and valuables, along with insane telephone bills. The guilt feelings that assaulted her were unbearable. "A true artist," she recalled. She tried to think what it was, this black hole, this bottomless pit of need, of desire, of lack, that had appeared within her—and not only her. A dark void that actually called out for that cruel hand to invade it, to penetrate and dig and take more and more.

By the time the police entered the picture, there was not much more to be done than to sum up the details and tally the damages. The investigating officer was mildly amused by the story. What particularly interested him was a possible link to a similar imbroglio that had taken place in Tel Aviv, which had ended precisely the same week that Pascal appeared in Jerusalem. There, in a little square shared by two cafés on Ibn Gabirol Street, a black-haired youth had shown up one day, with eyes as blue as pools, who was described by the complainants as quite shy, and he had presented an unforgettable little skit about Adam and Eve. As an encore he had taken on the role of God. His name was Bernard, and he was French, and many remembered how he had said that even as a child he had dreamed of one day visiting Tel Aviv.

At the Port

Translated by Gabriel Blau

'm sitting in a café at the port writing a story called "Where My Life Is Going." The story is about my having no idea where my life is going or what to do with it. In front of me is a huge ship. Two sailors hang off the side, painting the ship's name in black letters: "W," "h," "e," "r," "e," . . . in short, the ship is called "Where Is My Life." A flag waves from the mast bearing only the word "Going."

The captain is standing on the bridge. His bright white uniform is complete with golden epaulets, a mustache, and a whistle. His gestures are edgy; clearly he wants to get going. The sailors, bustling on the deck, are also edgy, affected greatly by the captain's nervousness.

I progress in my writing. The story, "Where My Life Is Going" has a beginning (which, by the way, is quite moving) a middle, and now I'm agonizing over the end. I want it to be optimistic, light, maybe even funny. It just never comes out right.

As I pay the bill, I notice the ship "Where Is My Life" under the flag "Going" has already hoisted its anchor and is leaving port. I ask the waiter if it's possible to bring it back.

The waiter brings over the owner of the café. I throw a fit and he calls over the general director of the port.

Sitting with me, the general director listens attentively as I explain what's happening. I demand the immediate return of the ship or that I be brought out to it in a service boat. It's unthinkable, you'll agree with me, that "Where Is My Life" and its crew would sail under the flag "Going" without me. Very politely the general director explains that there's no possibility of the ship's return. Instead he offers me another beer on him.

I try to argue but the manager stands firm that international law holds that a ship that leaves does not return. Nothing can be done about it. I'm offered a pleasure ride on a small barge or a net of fresh carp.

I'm sad, but men don't cry. The manager consoles me by saying that my ship will come too. There's no telling what it will be called, but it will clearly be mine. And I believe him, I do, but make one more request, that he wait with me.

Who Will Die Last

Translated by Ilene Prusher

dea for a story. Grandma's tale, by way of the engraved fork that I inherited.

Idea for a movie. The girl I used to be. A mixture of my own memories and my thoughts about Dina.

Three containers of cottage cheese. Do laundry. Call Dindin.

I am recording this on the voice recorder I bought last week. I enter the elevator of the building of Big TV. Inside I turn my back to the mirror and count in my head all the men I've been with. Thirteen names in the space of eighteen floors. It's a kind of exercise. Once I would have gotten to maybe six or seven. But now, after I have gone up and down this elevator at least a thousand times, I am capable of recalling all of them. And I still have a second to turn around and fix my hair.

Next to Arnon's office, three people are already waiting. Bonnie, the secretary, gives me her million-dollar smile. It's not for show, it's real: that's how I label the smile that she puts out for anyone who brings big money here. But that doesn't mean I don't have to wait in line. It's always a hassle, getting in to see him. During all the times I've waited here, I've never had a single good idea.

Finally I enter. Arnon doesn't feign enthusiasm, and I love that in him: no posturing and no bullshit. That way you know where you stand, more or less.

"Whatcha got?"

"An idea," I say.

"I'm sure you have at least one," he grins. (Great: we're off on the right foot.)

"Plastic surgery."

"Very good," he says.

"Ten surgeons. Ten platforms on the street. A million dollars. Every surgeon needs to convince as many women as possible to go under the knife. Whatever, random girls. Doesn't matter where: nose, breasts, ankles. And from there we go directly to the operating room. Or even right there, in a connecting tent, with anesthesiologists and everything you need on hand. The camera is following every moment. Live broadcast. A million dollars."

"For the surgeon or the patient?"

"Half-half."

"Not bad. But it won't work. Next idea."

"Why won't it work?"

"Because they're already working on something similar. Heart surgery."

"Really? I haven't heard of it."

"You don't want to know. It's pretty disgusting."

"It's unbelievable what people are stooping to now. But never mind. Here's another idea."

"Talk to me."

"Ten competitors. Each one chooses an animal, any animal. They need to enter the skin of this animal, to live in its den say, for a month, and the camera follows them the whole time. One climbs a tree, another hibernates, another one picks out lice, they hunt, they're hunted, the works."

"With an expert commenting?"

"No, just zoologists and anthropologists to give background information, on animal habitat, on comparisons between animals and human beings, things like that. What's beautiful about it will be when we get into the competitors' heads and hear their thoughts."

"How?"

"That's a technical problem. Just thoughts, not speech, not nonsense. Pure thoughts. If it's reality, we need to go all the way."

"You're stuck on animals, you." (That's a hint and maybe half a compliment. We filmed at the Biblical Zoo the reality show that I started five years ago, on account of which I made a name for myself. It began as a documentary film on people and their responses to the behavior of animals; it was a crazy success. The camera followed ten participants who stood for a full week across from an animal's cage, and they had to imitate its movements, day and night. Of course you must remember that one. The follow-up series was almost as successful: people in the cages, the animals outside.)

"What do you say?"

"Don't think so. Next."

"Why do you think there's a next?"

"You didn't come all this way without bringing something good. I know you." (Another one who says "I know you." My father, he's the one who started the trend, while I was still a baby. I know you. He doesn't know anything, my father, not even himself.)

"Okay. So here it is. 'Who Will Die First.'"

"Who will die first?"

"The name already justifies having a show, right?"

"Not bad. Go on."

"Ten participants. Five million dollars. Ten years. Who will die first?"

"What does it mean, who will die first, they kill each other?"

"Not really. It's actually got a very humanitarian undertone. Who will die first."

"Sorry, I don't get it."

"Ten participants. Five million dollars. Ten years. Locked in the house. The cameras wait patiently. Talking about life. Talking about death. Betting all the time, who will die first."

"So?"

"So someone will have a heart attack."

"Okay . . ."

"It's great drama, right?"

"Maybe. And then what happens?"

"He doesn't die."

"So what's the point?"

"That's the whole thing. We're not doing anything. It happens on its own. It so happens, with this guy's heart he's gonna live another twenty years."

"So who dies?"

"Someone will die eventually!"

"Why should somebody die?"

"Because that's life!"

"Die from what?"

"From whatever people die of! Cancer, okay? AIDS. Stroke. Someone will die!"

"And then?"

"Then they wait for the next . . ."

"Who will also die?"

"Eventually someone else will die, right?"

"Yes, but if everyone is young and beautiful, why would they die within ten years?"

"Then forget ten years. Twenty."

"I think I'm starting to get it."

"Or thirty. Whatever it takes."

"And whoever is left . . ."

"Gets the 5 million."

"Plus interest."

"Exactly."

"Thirty years, it could be a huge sum."

"I knew you'd go for it."

"I'm not going for anything yet. Why does it need to be on one location? It'll be a little boring after a year or two, no?"

"Oh, so that's the thing. I have an improved version. It follows the people throughout their lives. To their places of work. In each of their houses. We won't interfere at all in their daily lives. That's the power of this idea. We let them live their lives. In essence playing a bit with this matter of life and death: You think that you're alive? Yes, today you're alive. But tomorrow. . . ."

"Not bad. It's original. But why ten people?"

"Oh, I've thought of that. Not ten people. A hundred people. A thousand people. It can be a big production."

"I like the way you think. A thousand people. Thirty years."

"Go outside the box." (Both of us smile.) "More." (He looks at me in disbelief.)

"You mean . . ."

"Everybody. Not thirty years. All their lives. All their deaths. All over the world. All possible worlds."

"Bingo. We're going with this one. Be here tomorrow morning, we'll have a meeting with Haim and Anat. Just one thing."

"Yes?"

"The name . . ."

"'Who Will Die First'?"

"'Who Will Die Last.'"

I go out to the street, leave the car in the parking lot. It's raining. It doesn't bother me. I walk around to the back of the building, sit down by the wall, and watch a small water-fall that's splashing over a few stones. The water falls and falls, and I get a bit wet, but there's something beautiful here. . . . I am reminded of everything I have been through. All my documentary films. The good reviews. The not-so-good reviews. I couldn't pay my bills, but it didn't matter. Art is art. And today, too, it doesn't bother me. The money's fab but it's not the main thing. It's still art, and let someone come and tell me it isn't.

About the Translators

Marianna Barr ("The Life and Death of Frank 22" and "On the Porch") is a freelance literary translator of prose and poetry. She lives in Jerusalem.

Gabriel Blau ("At the Port") lives in New York with his husband and son. He is an activist and teacher in the LGBT Jewish community, currently serving as director of development and communications at Congregation Beit Simchat Torah.

Charlie Buckholtz ("To the Limit" and "That Boy") has coauthored several books of nonfiction, including *In Heaven Everything Is Fine: The Unsolved Life of Peter Ivers and the Lost History of New Wave Theatre* and *The God Who Hates Lies: Confronting and Rethinking Jewish Tradition*. He is senior editor at the Shalom Hartman Institute.

Ken Frieden ("Vadim," "The National Library," and "Sushi") has translated nonfiction and fiction from French, German, Hebrew, and Yiddish. In the 1980s, he translated essays by Jacques Derrida and Walter Benjamin; more recently, he translated the short fiction by Abramovitsh (Mendele) and Peretz in his anthology *Classic Yiddish Stories* (Syracuse University Press, 2004).

Shalom Goldman ("Stars") teaches in the religion department at Duke University. His expertise is in the comparative study of the monotheistic faiths, and he has written a number of books on the topic. His online essays on religion in the public sphere appear regularly at ReligionDispatches. org. Among his artistic endeavors is the coauthorship of the opera *Akhnaten*, by Philip Glass.

Terri Klein ("Green Island" and "Alone") is a performance poet, actress, and playwright from Cromwell, Connecticut. She combined four of David Ehrlich's stories into a short play, *A Coffee with the Author* (2004), which was produced in Middletown, Connecticut. Terri is grateful to Sarah Rubinfeld for her help in translating some of David Ehrlich's stories.

Ben Lerman ("It's All Right") is an emergency physician and writer living in Berkeley, California, with his wife Judy and children Sam and Eliza.

Ilene Prusher ("Who Will Die Last") is a Jerusalem-based journalist and fiction writer. She teaches writing workshops and journalism courses, is working for the Israeli newspaper *Haaretz*, and writes a popular blog called "Primigravida." Her first novel, *A Baghdad Fixer*, was published in 2012 by Halban (UK).

Naomi Seidman ("The Store" and "Tuesday and Thursday Mornings") is Koret Professor of Jewish Culture and director of the Richard S. Dinner Center for Jewish Studies at the Graduate Theological Union. Her most recent book is *Faithful Renderings: Jewish-Christian Difference and the Politics of Translation* (University of Chicago Press, 2006).

Michael Swirsky ("Utterly Nameless") is a Jerusalem-based translator whose work has included books by prominent Hebrew writers such as S. Y. Agnon, Haim Gouri, and Adin Steinsaltz.

Michael Weingrad ("The Sol Popovitch War" and "On Reserve") is professor of Judaic Studies at Portland State University. He is the author of *American Hebrew Literature: Writing Jewish National Identity in the United States* (Syracuse University Press, 2011).

Chana Jenny Weisberg ("Lilly") is the creator of the popular website JewishMom.com and the author of two books, *Expecting Miracles* and *One Baby Step at a Time*.

Eva Weiss ("How the World Is Run") is a New York–born writer and editor who has lived in Jerusalem since 1992. Her work includes translating literary and academic projects.

About the Author
and Editor

David Ehrlich (born 1959) grew up in Ramat-Gan (near Tel-Aviv). After his military service, he became a journalist for *Ha-aretz* and the Israeli radio, among other media. For several years, he traveled in Greece, Australia, and the United States and taught Hebrew and Israeli culture at Emory University, Dartmouth College, and the University of California at Berkeley.

Ehrlich returned to Israel in 1993 and founded the bookstore café Tmol Shilshom. He runs the bookstore, teaches creative writing, and is a commentator and public speaker about Israeli society, culture, and literature. Ehrlich has been involved with LGBT activism and was one of the founders of the Israeli Aids Task Force. He currently lives with his two children in Jerusalem.

Ehrlich's two books of short stories in Hebrew, *Ha-bekarim shel shlishi ve-hamishi* (Tuesday and Thursday Mornings) and *Kahol 18* (Blue 18), were published in 1999 and 2003.

Ken Frieden has been the B. G. Rudolph Professor of Judaic Studies at Syracuse University since 1993. His books include *Classic Yiddish Fiction* (1995) and anthologies of literature in translation, such as *Tales of Mendele the Book Peddler* (1996) and *Classic Yiddish Stories* (2004). Previous translations from Hebrew he has edited include Aharon Appelfeld's short story "Badenheim 1939" and Miron Izakson's novel *Nathan and His Wives*. He has been a visiting professor and research fellow at universities from Tel Aviv, Haifa, and Jerusalem to Berlin, Heidelberg, and Harvard. Since 1996 he has edited (with Harold Bloom) the series *Judaic Traditions in Literature, Music, and Art* at Syracuse University Press.